The CUPID Company

First published in Great Britain by HarperCollins
Children's Books 2009
HarperCollins *Children's Books* is a division of
HarperCollins*Publishers* Ltd,
77-85 Fulham Palace Road, Hammersmith, London W6 8JB

Visit us on the web at
www.harpercollins.co.uk

2

THE CUPID COMPANY, It Takes Two
Text copyright © HarperCollins *Children's Books* 2009

Amber Aitken asserts the moral right to be identified
as the author of this work.

ISBN-13 978 0 00 731349 5

Printed and bound in England by
Clays Ltd, St Ives plc

Mixed Sources
Product group from well-managed
forests and other controlled sources
www.fsc.org Cert no. SW-COC-1806
© 1996 Forest Stewardship Council
FSC

FSC is a non-profit international organisation established to promote the
responsible management of the world's forests. Products carrying the FSC
label are independently certified to assure consumers that they come
from forests that are managed to meet the social, economic and
ecological needs of present and future generations.

Find out more about HarperCollins and the environment at
www.harpercollins.co.uk/green

Amber Aitken

The CUPID Company

It Takes Two

HarperCollins *Children's Books*

To the Winksie sisters

the gift of love

Coral was spread out flat on her bed, knees up, making a pointy P-shape, when her mother knocked on her bedroom door. She had had a bath and was in her pyjamas watching a romantic comedy she'd already seen over twenty times. There were hearts on her duvet, hearts on her curtains... even small pink heart-shaped fairy lights draped all across her headboard. Just like her bedroom, Coral's life had a theme: she was totally in love with love. It really made her world turn.

Coral's mum came in, smiling that dreamy sort of smile mothers sometimes have when you're not in trouble or being ordered to do something. She sat down on the bed, when suddenly there was a loud yelp. The duvet came alive, rising up and wriggling in the air. Coral's mum shrieked and leaped just as high. A black blotch of a nose emerged from beneath the duvet, followed by a white shaggy face and dark brown eyes floating in pools the colour of dark chocolate. There were two small flaps of caramel ears and another patch across the belly, but the rest of the dog's body was white – or it was supposed to be. This, though, depended on a number of things: whether he'd been taking flying jumps at muddy puddles, rolling in washed-up seaweed, or tumbling through burrs. He was a dog with many active pursuits. This was how Coral usually explained it to her mum, who never seemed particularly impressed.

"You nearly crushed Romeo," Coral grumbled.

"Coral – I have told you before. Romeo is not to sleep on your bed." Coral's mum looked serious. She pointed to the dog basket, positioned neatly below a large poster of two swans with their long necks curved into a heart shape, and stared sternly at the Jack Russell.

Romeo knew which bed was his. The patchwork dog's eyes dipped pitifully and glanced pleadingly from the pointed finger to the stern face.

"Romeo. NOW!" Coral's mum ordered.

Quickly the dog scampered off the bed and bounced like a ball into his basket. He rested his chin on one paw, tucked the other over his head and pretended to go to sleep, although he was really thinking doggy thoughts.

Coral frowned and blew noisily at the red-brown curl which had fallen across her eyes. She much preferred Romeo snuggled up against her.

"I have something for you," her mum revealed as she pushed a small brown envelope across the bed.

Coral wiggled upright and reached for the offering. Her name looped in curly writing across the front. Pressing the envelope gently, she could feel something hard and long. Carefully, she opened it.

Inside was a key and a note from her Great-Aunt Coral – after whom she'd been named.

Dear girl,

Weren't we the special pair – one of us a namesake and the other a great-aunt! Here is the key to Coral Hut. I thought it only right that my beach hut and all its treasures should go to you. I've enjoyed watching you grow; you've got a good head

for romance. We shared more than you know.

I trust that you will look after and cherish Coral Hut, just as I have done all these years. It has been my very favourite place in the world. Make it yours.

Sincerely yours,

Great-Aunt Coral

Coral Hut, No. 5 the Promenade, Sunday Harbour

Coral reread the note. The words 'beach hut' fizzled in her memory. Now that she thought about it, she remembered her mother once mentioning that her Great-Aunt Coral owned a beach hut down at the harbour. The key was long and black and cold in Coral's hand. She looked to her mother for confirmation.

"Coral Hut is all yours," she nodded, smiling.

Coral thought about the colourful wooden beach huts lined up on the harbour like crabs with their long skinny legs pushed deep into the sand. She could find her way there with her eyes shut. Down to Café Cod. Through the cobbled alleys and behind the wooden-clad houses painted white and pale blue. Past Blades restaurant and the fragrant fish market stalls nestled in between the small upturned fishing boats, sheets of torn nets and piles of old lobster pots. Beyond the south quay, along the beach past the old jetty – yes, there stood Sunday Harbour's own row of beach huts. Coral could almost smell the salt air already. She tried to imagine number five in the row.

"For me?" she finally wondered out loud.

"That's right."

"When can I see it?"

Her mum shrugged. "Tomorrow, I guess."

"Morning?"

"It's your summer holiday – you can go any time you like."

Her mum had a point. There was no school for weeks. Coral had her friends. And her very own beach hut!

"I must phone Nicks," she squealed. She also needed to remember to breathe.

Her mum laughed. "Fine, but make it quick. It's getting late."

Like she was going to sleep anyway. But Coral's mum wouldn't want to hear that.

"Oh, yes, quick, quick," she agreed as she scrambled out of bed and dashed into the hallway. She headed for the unpainted straight-back chair pushed up close to the wall and settled on to its hard tapestry cushion. It was not a comfortable arrangement, but her father liked it just so.

Just above her a wall-mounted phone shared space with a gold and dark wood hanging frame. But the frame didn't hold a photograph or a pretty mounted picture. Instead, typed in simple black bold, were the words: PHONECALLS COST. KEEP IT CHEAP & CHEERFUL. Her father was a watcher of bills. He was an accountant; he couldn't help himself. But at that moment Coral had far more important things to think about.

Reaching for the cordless handset, she punched in Nicks's number while staring up at the ceiling. She could dial her best friend's number without looking. It was a little game she played with herself (it was probably an only-child thing). Nicks answered on the eighth ring.

"Hello?"

"What took you so long!" Coral cried out passionately. Her news – stuck inside her for so long – had practically knotted up her intestines.

"Oh, hi, Coral," replied Nicks evenly. "I was just getting ready for bed."

Of course she was. But Coral was too excited to think sensibly. Her thoughts were a high-speed blur. She tried to snatch the words zooming around her head and place them into sentences, but it would have taken too long. So she simply caught them and threw them out, one by one.

"I have. Well. Actually. My Great-Aunt

Coral. She gave me. Or left me. A beach hut. It's mine!"

The phone was silent for a few moments.

"What beach hut?"

Coral was fizzing with excitement and had expected Nicks's reaction to be just as delirious. Dumped back down to earth, she tried again.

"My great-aunt owned a beach hut," she explained, slowing her pace. "It was her favourite place until she became very old. And now it's mine."

"Yours?"

"Seems so."

"Really?"

"Definitely. It's even called Coral Hut!"

Coral was suddenly very grateful that her parents hadn't named her after Hildegard, her great-aunt on her mum's side. Actually she was grateful for more than one reason.

"Wow, that is brilliant!" Nicks cried out gleefully.

"I know! And we can go and see it tomorrow morning."

"Tomorrow? Double brilliant." That was Nicks excited. She just wasn't the squealing type. "So what does it look like?"

"Uh, I don't really know."

"I bet it's ace!"

Coral closed her eyes and built a beach hut in her mind. It was cute and colourful and very girly and all their friends would think they were amazing for having it. She was so busy imagining it she forgot all about Nicks... until her father threw his deep voice like a bowling ball down the hallway. *"Say good night, Coral!"*

That knocked her out of her daydream.

"See you tomorrow morning very early, Nicks," Coral whispered. "Good night."

She didn't know about a good night, but it would certainly be a long one. She climbed back into bed and snuggled up to the warm hairy bundle beside her. Life was good. Even Romeo's doggy breath didn't seem quite so bad.

love nest

"Coral, have some breakfast, please."

"But Nicks is waiting for me!"

Coral's mum pushed a piece of toast with honey into her hand. "Well, eat it on the way then." She inspected her daughter's head of crazy curls and reached for her handbag. "You haven't even brushed your hair."

Coral faked left and bolted right. But she wasn't quick enough. She was suddenly in the midst of an energetic hairbrushing. Nicks's neatly combed blonde head peered round the kitchen door.

"There's toast made, Nicks," advised Coral's mum.

"I've already had scrambled eggs, thank you." Nicks smiled.

Coral scowled. What did breakfast matter when the beach hut was waiting? Romeo chewed at her laces. He knew something was up and he was just as eager to find out what.

Finally – released from the brush – Coral and her two best friends made a swift dash for the beach, flying down alleys and past houses in a blur. Finally they arrived at a neat row of beach huts standing one beside the other in a straight, sea-facing queue. Of course the girls had seen the huts before, but things were different now. The beach huts were all the same, but they weren't. One of these huts was now *theirs*.

The slice of toast in Coral's fingers had

gone cold and soggy. It wasn't designed for breaking land-speed records. She ignored it and stared with eyes like two shiny coins, her mouth open and round, ready to ooh and aah as soon as she found Coral Hut. Nicks's gaze too was fixed on the huts. Romeo, though, was more interested in the toast. He stood up on his back legs and nibbled around Coral's fingers.

The huts all had narrow double doors with windows on either side. Every single one had a small deck with a railing and sloping roof. And yet each beach hut was different. Some were colourful. Others were plain. Some had their own fancy features like wagon-wheel deck railings and carved wooden window shutters.

"What number did you say Coral Hut was?" asked Nicks with a wrinkled-up face. The bright early-morning sunshine dazzled her.

"Number five," Coral called out as she counted.

Nicks used one hand to shade her eyes and pointed with the other. "That must be it then."

Coral followed her finger. But that hut was dull. It was nothing but bare, bleached wood. There was nothing special about that hut.

Coral mooched over to it. The key slipped in first time. She breathed in sharply. Now all she had to do was to open the double doors. She glanced over at Nicks nervously. Her friend shrugged and smiled: it was only a beach hut. She nodded – and pushed. Inside, the beach hut couldn't have been more different...

It was a breathtaking, girly heaven. So there were cobwebs, but she could see through those. Coral did a quick whizz-around the small room and then started back at the beginning, sucking in each detail and swallowing it down like a sweet treat. Everywhere was light and summery, with wooden walls whitewashed in cottagey-white.

Coral smiled. There was a white wrought-iron daybed pressed against one wall with a sturdy, pink-painted straight chair to serve as a table beside it. On its seat was a white enamel jug of flower stalks. Rose petals had fallen and dried around its base. Coral's smile widened. In the middle of the floor lay a rug of pink primroses. Stencilled roses scrambled along the edges of the exposed white wooden floor. There was a white wicker basket nestled in one corner. Her eyes darted back to the daybed, covered in cushions of pretty pastel prints and rambling roses, floral gingham and woven checks. One wall had a shelf filled with books. Three gold picture frames hung on the opposite wall. Coral's smile was now so wide it was almost reaching her ears. It was the dreamiest, most beautiful place she'd ever seen. Or it would be, once they'd cleared away all the dust and cobwebs.

Finally, she dragged her happy eyes back

over to her friend. Nicks met her gaze. They wore matching faces.

"Woo-hoo!" they both shrieked ecstatically. And Nicks was not the shrieking sort.

"And it's all ours!" Coral added by way of a second shriek. Of course it was all theirs. They shared everything. Romeo growled at a spider running for cover and then barked at a nosy seagull who had perched himself on the deck railing, eager to take a look at the hut's new inhabitants.

Nicks giggled. "Well, come on then." She grabbed Coral's hand and together they tumbled inside the little piece of beachy heaven that was Coral Hut.

Nicks made immediately for the shelves on the wall to inspect the books while Coral went towards the white wicker basket tucked into a cosy corner. She swiped at a dust layer and hoisted the lid. Inside there were two enamel candle holders, one pale blue and the other a butter-yellow colour, with a small box of candles. Next there was a large, flat paisley box of scented paper and pens. Coral brought her nose closer to the paper. The sheets smelled of perfumed musk that reminded her of Great-Aunt Coral. She gave one more sniff before putting the paper down and picking up a cake tin printed with cherry blossoms. Would it smell just as good inside? She prised off its lid. It was empty but smelled of roses, like it might once have held squares of Turkish delight. It was a pretty little tin and so Coral set it to one side. It deserved to sit on top of the wicker basket, not inside lost in the darkness.

Suddenly, Nicks called her over excitedly, which put an end to Coral's searching and sniffing through the basket for that day.

"You must look at this!" Nicks had an open book in one hand and was looking at the three gold-framed pictures on the wall. Coral scurried over. The frames were filled with prints of chubby cupids with curly hair and feathery wings. One cupid held a harp in its fat little fingers; another had a small horn plumping up its cheeks.

"And listen to this." Nicks blew at the dust on the book and began reading out loud. "*Oh my love is like a red, red rose that's newly sprung in June; oh my love is like the melody that's sweetly played in tune.*" Nicks grinned and flicked a few pages forward in the book and continued to read. "*How do I love thee? Let me count the ways. I love thee to the depth and breadth and height my soul can reach.*"

Coral wondered what Nicks was on about. Her face must have said it all.

"It's a book of romantic poetry," Nicks explained. "And there are lots more just like it – look!" The shelf above her head was heavy with books all crowded up against one another.

Coral gazed from the books to the cupids. Coral Hut was like a temple to love. She remembered her great-aunt's note; who'd have ever guessed that the old lady was the romantic sort? What a pity there hadn't been enough time to get to know her better...

Nicks found two faded, folded deckchairs and dragged them out on to the deck, although there was no way she could sit down yet. She gazed out blissfully at the ocean. She could also see the lifeboat station and the cobbled launching jetty. Sunday Harbour pier was a stripe in the distance. It was early in the day, but the beach was already busy with people and dogs and boats. Coral meanwhile scurried between the hut and deck. She couldn't stop moving; it was all way too exciting.

"Look – throws for snuggling under!" she exclaimed, cheerfully chucking a candy-striped woven blanket at her friend. They'd been hidden under the daybed. Nicks disappeared beneath a cloud of dust.

"Just what I don't need!" She coughed and

laughed and Coral vanished inside the hut again. But Nicks stayed outdoors to have a look at the huts on either side of theirs. The one to their right was painted khaki and had camouflage netting thrown over its roof. The hut to their left was simpler and painted a bold glossy red. They'd been in such a hurry to discover Coral Hut that they hadn't paid any attention to their neighbours. Both huts stood silent and locked up tight.

Just then a familiar face caught Nicks's eye. Actually, it was two familiar faces. They were laughing, and then they shared a kiss.

"Coral – get out here, quick!" Nicks called.

Coral instantly appeared, breathless and with wild hair. The combination of sea air and energetic poking around had sent her curls crazy.

Nicks pointed at the water's edge. "Look."

An old man wearing swimming trunks and goggles was doing star jumps. Two women went speed-walking by with their elbows

24

flying like pistons. A small girl with a head of colourful glitter clips collected shells. But most important of all – a young man and woman stood and kissed...

love relations

There was a reason why Nicks and Coral were so pleased at the sight of the kissing couple. But to understand why meant going back in time to the beginning... to the day of Great-Aunt Coral's funeral... to the day it all began...

:

It was one o'clock in the afternoon and Coral was staring at the sandwich on her plate. The bread was wholewheat and nutty. Brown bird-feed bread; it was not her favourite. And one edge was hard and crusty. What was the point of crusts? She'd often wondered the same about homework. Prising open the sandwich, she stared at the dissolving egg mayo inside. It was nothing personal, but egg mayo was simply not a summer sort of sandwich filler. Now a choccie biscuit – that was a summer sort of tummy filler! She turned to the small side table. But there was not a single choccie thing in sight, and not a single biscuit left on her plate. Her eyes kept moving until they landed on Nicks's plate. Her friend was munching on what looked suspiciously like a choccie biscuit.

Nicks looked up. "You're staring at me, Coral," she said, scratching her head with a face like it hurt.

"And *you're* eating my choccie biscuit."

"I'm *sharing* your biscuit," said Nicks, offering it back to her friend.

Coral made a huffy face, so Nicks took another nibble and made a delicate lip-smacking sound. "Fine," was all she said.

There was no reasoning with a biscuit guzzler. So Coral shifted her attention to the rest of the people in the living room. They were all very busy eating, moving around and talking. She watched Nicks's mother nodding gently while she listened to a group of ladies dressed smartly in brooches and hats. She ran the local post office and knew almost everyone. Coral's own mother strolled around the room doling out stuffed eggs, mini muffins and biscuits for dunking. She made pint-sized chit-chat as she moved, always offering a smile with a small sympathetic tilt of her head. *No, it just won't be the same without Great-Aunt Coral. Oh yes, she will be dearly missed.*

"It's nice that your family has come together to remember Great-Aunt Coral," Nicks said.

Coral nodded.

"Are you OK?" Nicks's face was worried.

Coral nodded. The old lady was not much more than a picture in her head. She was twelve years old and yet in all that time she'd never really spent much time with her great-aunt.

Nicks was staring at her friend. "Coral, are you sure you're all right?"

Actually, she was starving. She stared mournfully at the egg mayo growing mould on her plate. "I guess I'll be fine, Nicks."

"Shall I get you something?"

She nodded. "A sandwich, please. And I could probably do with one of those mini-muffin things too."

"Yes, of course." Nicks nodded and headed for Coral's mum and the travelling plate of snacks.

Coral remained perched on her hard chair and stared out across the room. Her grandfather had fallen asleep in his chair. An aunt (of the non-great variety) was scraping sponge cake off the fake Persian carpet. Her father was standing over a very small cousin who seemed determined to reach the handmade miniature sailing boats on the mantelpiece. Her father had dedicated months to the building of those little boats. And then her cousin Archie wafted in through the front door like a south-westerly sea breeze. He was alone.

Archie was eighteen – nine years older than Coral – and he still hadn't got himself a girlfriend. Coral blamed the rock climbing. After all, what girlfriend wanted to watch rock climbing? Archie even did fake rock climbing, or that's what it seemed to Coral – climbing pretend rock walls in sports centres.

Coral waved as Archie passed, but he was on course for the kitchen so she searched for Nicks again.

Her best friend seemed to be talking to a thin young woman with long, dark hair tied in a loose bun. Her eyes were red circles and matched her blotchy cheeks. Coral's mum's head was once again tilted with sympathy. She reached for the small plate in Nicks's hands and offered a biscuit to the sad woman, who accepted one, taking a dainty bite. The biscuit seemed to calm her. Nicks leaned over and rubbed the young woman's shoulders like she was caught in a blizzard and needed to stay warm...

When Nicks did finally return, Coral was still in her chair and listening to her godmother's second rendition of the Begonia Story (she'd planted what she thought were begonia seeds only to discover that there must have been some mix-up because yellow daisies had grown instead). Coral laughed anyway.

Her godmother spied Nicks and sighed. "Nicks, darling, thank goodness," she cried, looking quite relieved. "The sausage rolls are ready – only I couldn't bear to see dear Coral sitting here all on her own." And then she was gone. Coral shrugged. She understood. This was not the sort of day for anybody to be sitting alone.

"Who were you talking to?" she asked her best friend.

"That's Gwyn," Nicks replied. "Gwyn was your great-aunt's homecare nurse. She'd been with her for almost two years. She's taking all this quite badly."

Coral nodded sympathetically and tried to catch Gwyn's attention. The homecare nurse finally saw Coral's smile and returned it sadly. She was wedged in between the rhubarb tarts at the edge of the food table and another blue-rinsed relative who was also asleep in a chair. Coral wondered if some company might cheer her up. The snoring wasn't very cheery. And the rhubarb tarts didn't seem to be doing it either.

Archie, she noticed, was now at the other end of the food table and looked lost.

Rock-climbing audiences had dwindled since all the old folks had started nodding off one by one. He was standing with his hands in his pockets, gazing about the room, looking for something interesting to focus on. The wall behind him finally caught his attention and he pulled a hand from his pocket and rapped it with his knuckles. Coral watched her cousin carefully. He was examining the wall for its climbing potential! Somebody had to save him.

"What about Archie and Gwyn?" she whispered to Nicks.

'What do you mean 'what about them'?'" Her best friend shrugged and nodded. "Individually or as a couple?"

'As a couple, of course," Coral grinned.

Nicks turned sharply. The girls' noses now touched. "You're not thinking of playing matchmaker, are you?"

Coral was thinking of doing precisely that. But she kept her face blank. "Uh, not really.

But it does look as if they could both do with a bit of company, doesn't it?"

"Coral, this is a wake – not Valentine's Day." Nicks looked stern.

"I have been remembering my great-aunt all day," Coral mumbled in self-defence. She had only just been wondering why the old lady had never married or had children. "I just think it might be nice for Archie and Gwyn to meet."

Nicks's face softened slightly. "An arranged meeting, you mean?"

Now she looked vaguely interested.

"I have a very small plan – it's barely even an introduction."

Finally Nicks gave in. "Oh, all right, tell me about it," she said.

And Coral did, in detail. She needed her friend's help. Nicks listened carefully and sprinkled a few sighs on the plan. She hadn't counted on being dragged in to help. But finally she agreed.

Coral went first. She approached the food table and the plate of chocolate éclairs. There were four left. She stood with her feet slightly apart and her shoulders square, and ate three one after the other. She paused for a short moment at that point, chocolate, pastry and whipped cream fighting for space inside her. She felt her stomach shudder and inflate. There was a chance it might burst. She braced herself, but the moment passed. She would be OK.

Dabbing at her whipped cream moustache with an orange paper serviette, she gave Nicks the thumbs up. There was no time to waste. She made her way over to cousin Archie, who was now inspecting the ceiling. Perhaps this rock climber thought he was Spider-Man.

"Hi, Arch," she said.

His eyes dropped from the ceiling and landed on her. "Hi, small fry," he answered.

"You've got to try the éclairs, Archie," she

declared, like a life might depend on it.

"I do, huh?"

"Oh, yes! They. Are. Amazing. Definitely the best I've ever tasted."

Archie nodded. "OK, sure." But he didn't move. He didn't even budge. Coral stared at him expectantly. Did he expect waiter service?

"You have to get one now," she pleaded, swallowing hard. The third éclair was fighting her. "There's only one left. It's now or never, believe me. The word is out."

Her cousin looked a little perplexed and then finally shuffled his feet. "If you say so," was all he said as he turned for the food table.

This was only one half of the plan. Coral searched for Nicks, who was now with Gwyn. She glanced over at Archie. He was almost at the éclairs. Would there be enough time?

Nicks was still talking. Gwyn was still listening. Now Archie was at the food table.

Finally Gwyn stood up. Nicks looked

relieved and scurried back over to her friend. And together they watched the rest.

Gwyn stood over the food table and spied the éclair just as Archie reached for it.

"Oh, I am sorry," she said apologetically.

Archie glanced from the éclair to Gwyn's face. "Were you after the éclair?"

"No, no, you have it."

"Please – go ahead," urged Archie.

"You were here first." Gwyn smiled coyly.

Archie grinned back. "Ladies first," he reminded her.

"We could share it?"

Archie turned the idea over in his head and nodded. He reached for a knife and made a clean, precise cut down the middle. "I've been told they're really delicious," he said as he handed Gwyn her half.

She seemed surprised. "Oh, my, I've heard the same. They must be really good then."

They took bites with smiling mouths and watched each other over chocolate-coated pastry. Neither seemed in a hurry to move on.

Nicks and Coral turned and gave each other fierce hugs.

all you need is love

So there you go. That was the start of it – the day the Cupid Company was born. The girls decided then and there to make it their mission to matchmake other loveless people in Sunday Harbour. Nobody loved love more than Coral and Nicks. And they had, after all, successfully played matchmaker to Archie and Gwyn (the couple kissing on the beach at that very moment!). So it really was their destiny.

Coral turned and faced her friend with a big grin. "What a result!"

"What a pair of matchmakers we are," agreed Nicks with an identical grin.

Coral thought about it some more. "You know, there's a chance I may have a special talent," she added. After all, Archie and Gwyn had been her idea. She then thought about Great-Aunt Coral. Was this talent something she'd inherited? After all, Coral Hut was like a shrine to love. Coral Hut. That was it! Coral tapped her chin thoughtfully. It seemed like the universe was sending them a message.

She stared at Nicks, but she was focused on Romeo, who had disappeared on to the beach and returned with a plastic spade in his mouth.

"Maybe it's actually Great-Aunt Coral who is sending us a message from... wherever she is," Coral wondered out loud. "Maybe the beach hut is where she wants our company to be – where we should base it all. This could be our Cupid Company head office!"

'What a brilliant idea!' said Nicks excitedly. 'But just how do we find more people to matchmake?' she murmured thoughtfully.

Coral hadn't thought that part through. But her enthusiasm was gathering speed. She felt a bit like Venus – the goddess of love (and probably Cupid's cousin or something). "We'll work it out. It'll be all for love and love for all!" she cried out passionately.

"It will?"

"Yes, that can be the Cupid Company's motto."

Nicks was contemplative for a moment. "Mmm. If we're going to do this then we must do it properly. We should have questionnaires for the Cupid Company clients to fill out – you know, listing their likes and dislikes. That way we know who to match up."

"Good idea," agreed Coral.

"And we'll need to distribute some Cupid Company posters. Every company needs to advertise. And of course we'll have to clean Coral Hut up properly. We'll probably need to paint the outside too. It'll make a far better impression."

Now all Nicks needed was a clipboard to write all those useful points down. She was a top organiser. And if she was going to be the head of the Cupid Company then Coral was definitely the heart. They really were the perfect pair.

"But before we do anything," Nicks paused with a finger planted firmly in the air, "we need to return this spade to its rightful owner."

Coral glanced down at Romeo, who still had the plastic spade gripped tightly in his mouth. She nodded happily. And even though they were only matching a missing spade with a child, already she felt like the fairy godmother of happy endings.

labour of love

It was not even lunchtime, but already it felt like the end of the day. The girls had arrived at Coral Hut early that morning weighed down with buckets, soap and thick sponges. Even Romeo had carried a feather duster in his mouth. They'd certainly started off with great gusto. But cleaning the beach hut had only seemed like fun for a while. After that it was just plain old cleaning.

Coral's mum arrived just in time. Not only did she have sandwiches, chocolate bars and a large bag of cleaned laundry, but the girls knew she'd offer to help them. One of the girls counted on it.

"Mum!" cried Coral. "Oh, thank goodness. I am pooped!" She laid her palm across her forehead and closed her eyes just to prove it. There was even a chance she might faint. Probably. Or at least maybe. She thought she'd better sit down.

"So are you done then?" wondered her mum.

Nicks stood holding a sponge with bubbles up to her elbow. "Nope." She eyed Coral. "We still have the floor to do."

Coral thought it was time to change the subject. "Did you bring the paint with you?"

"Your father offered to buy that," her mum replied. "He'll bring it over later."

Coral frowned. Mr Keep-it-Cheap-and-Cheerful was off buying their paint? This was not necessarily good news.

"He does know we want pink paint, doesn't he?"

Her mum nodded distractedly and opened a bag of clean laundry. She hauled out cushion and daybed covers – all clean and fresh and cobweb free. She stacked them in a tall towering pile on one of the deckchairs, and only when she was finished did she acknowledge the lump that was Coral slumped on the floor.

"I'll make a deal with you," she began. Coral perked up slightly. "You finish the floor and I'll put all the clean covers back on for you."

Coral wilted. She'd hoped that the deal would include an offer to do the floor. But finally she nodded. And, like her mum, she kept her promise. She tried her best too, although Nicks didn't seem to see it that way. But Coral couldn't help it if her friend was super-speedy with a sponge. She had one speed and this was it.

When Coral's mum left, the girls were stretched out and lolling with their tired hands and feet dangling from their deckchairs. They were out of energy and simply sat and stared out at the people on the beach. Junior lifeguards raced between orange cones. A surfer rubbed wax on to his surfboard. And the same small girl they'd seen earlier – the one with the colourful glitter clips in her hair – collected more shells. Only this time she had two ponytails with a whole bunch of scrunchies in each one, making her ponytails stand out straight like tentacles.

"There's that little girl collecting shells again," noticed Nicks.

"We should definitely call her Shelly," decided Coral as she sank deeper into her deckchair.

Nicks was silent for a few moments. She sat upright. "That's enough lying about; we really should get busy! We've got Cupid

Company posters to make and questionnaires to write." There was no time for hanging around – not if they were going to do this properly. And Nicks only did things one way, and that was properly.

Coral still hadn't recovered from the cleaning. She yawned. "But my dad will be here soon with the paint." Or he could be. There was every chance that he might be. So there was no sense in starting anything else. But Nicks had already disappeared in the direction of the wicker basket. She returned with sheets of scented paper and a few coloured pens.

"Let's start with the questionnaire," she suggested. "And then we'll make a few Cupid Company posters." She armed herself with a pen and put the end in her mouth to help her think better. "Now, apart from the basics like name and age and *boy or girl*, what else shall we include on this questionnaire?"

Coral sat upright. She had recovered from

the cleaning marathon; she was back in Cupid Company mode. Ideas were definitely her thing. "There should be a section for hobbies," she suggested brightly. "And likes and dislikes. Mmm. Better leave a few lines for strange habits too. You know what I mean..." She smirked at her friend knowingly.

"What is that supposed to mean?" demanded Nicks.

"You practise silent kung fu when you're concentrating."

"Well, you put ketchup on everything."

"You sleep with the covers over your head."

"You hum to yourself all the time."

The girls stared at each other, silent. And then they exploded with laughter.

"I'd better include quite a few empty lines for strange habits then," agreed Nicks. "What about star signs? A lot of people think they count for something."

Coral nodded. "And we'd better include a bit at the bottom, saying something like: 'I swear this is the truth, the whole truth and nothing but the truth'. And they must sign it too."

"This is the Cupid Company, Coral, not a courtroom," snorted her friend.

"Trust me, Nicks; you just can't be too careful out there."

The girls stared thoughtfully at the questionnaire.

"Right, that's done then," said Nicks. "Now for the Cupid Company poster." She took out a clean sheet of paper and handed it to Coral. "Your turn."

Coral did like to make her mark. She knew exactly what she thought the poster should say too. First, she wrote: *THE CUPID COMPANY – ALL FOR LOVE AND LOVE FOR ALL*. And then she drew two hearts overlapping. Below this she wrote: *We Are Your Matchmaking Specialists. Find Love and Live Happily Ever After. Our Work is Guaranteed.*

Nicks waited until she was done. "But it's not really, is it?"

"Not really what?"

"Guaranteed."

"Oh, everyone says that. It's just advertising talk."

"But we're matchmakers, not plumbers. You can't guarantee love."

It was just like Nicks to pooh-pooh her ideas. So Coral ignored her and drew another poster, just like the last one. Nicks picked up her own clean sheet of paper and drew a poster too, only she left out the bit about their matchmaking services being guaranteed. They were silent while they drew, and before long they had at least ten posters between them.

"If we're going to put posters up around Sunday Harbour we may as well hand out a few questionnaires to our friends at the same time," suggested Nicks sensibly. "So we'll need to make a few more of those too."

Coral frowned and stretched her aching fingers. "More questionnaires? Mmm. You get started… I won't be long." She slumped into her deckchair.

Coral was excitable, but it wasn't the long-lasting kind. Nicks knew this better than anyone. "We could stop by the post office on the way. I'm sure my mum will make photocopies of the questionnaire for us," she suggested as she gathered herself up. It was handy having a mum who ran the post office. It also meant that they always had the best Christmas postage stamps for their cards.

Coral suddenly jumped up too. "You're brilliant, Nicks! We've got far more important things to see to, anyway." She grinned at her friend, who replied with a harrumph.

"She's only making a few photocopies," Nicks said with a sigh. Give Coral five minutes and she'd probably talk Nicks's mum into helping them put the posters up too. She was possibly the most persuasive girl in Sunday Harbour!

Coral nodded agreeably and stood with her hands on the deck railings as she surveyed the beach. She was considering some of the best places in Sunday Harbour for their posters. From the post office they could trot down to the lifeguards' station. Come to think of it, Reggie who ran it usually went everywhere with his two brothers. They were always laughing, fooling about and playing pranks on each another. But it was probably time he met Mrs Reggie. It was just what you did when you got older. Coral made a mental note to hand him a questionnaire.

Further along from the lifeguard's station stood the community notice board. Mr Gelatti's ice-cream van was always parked alongside it. And he always drew a crowd. There had to be an empty space for their poster on the notice board. This got her thinking about Mr Gelatti. He needed someone to keep him company while he sold ice cream; life inside an ice-cream van could be a lonely one. He definitely needed a questionnaire too.

Of course they could also stop by the Seaside Store with its cotton sundresses and straw hats in the window. And what about the Treasure Chest, where they sold jewellery made out of shells. She'd seen posters in their window too. The Sundog Art Gallery also had notices and advertisements pinned to its front door. And Bicycles for Hire was only two doors down. Its manager was called Flat Tyre Francine and she was definitely the grumpiest person in Sunday Harbour. If anybody needed to find true love it was Flat Tyre Francine. Coral decided she would slip a questionnaire beneath the door of Bicycles for Hire too (they didn't dare step inside, not even for love). The Cupid Company was ready to launch.

love thy neighbour

Now that the girls had the beach hut, each new day seemed more exciting than the last. Romeo loved it there just as much too. He'd wake Coral up every morning very early by licking her head and growling softly in her ear. He was a very busy dog. He had seagulls to chase (from the hut's deck he could survey the beach and carefully select each bird for chasing). He had crabs to sniff out (even if he ran away as fast as a gale wind when he actually came across one). And he had fish to find (one day he would catch one for sure). So it was important he got to the beach early.

One day when the girls arrived at Coral Hut, their neighbours – the ones who owned the khaki-painted hut with the camouflage netting on the roof – were already there. There was a very tall man with shoulders as big and wide as a ship's lookout, and a woman who was as dainty as a sparrow. She noticed the girls and waved. He saluted.

"Well, hello there, neighbours!" the woman called out cheerily. For a small person she was particularly loud.

Of course the girls couldn't just saunter past. It was polite and neighbourly to stop by. So they drew up to the khaki hut, took a breath and opened their mouths – but the woman was much, much quicker.

"Welcome to Sunday Harbour's beach hut community!" she cried out. "One of you must be little Coral." Her eyes danced between the girls, but she didn't pause long enough for either of them to reply. "Oh, how we loved your great-aunt. She was so special. She will be missed. But it's lovely to have you as our new neighbours." Finally she seemed to run out of words.

"Hello, I'm Coral." Coral raised her hand in the air.

"And I'm Nicks."

"We're best friends," explained Coral, just in case the woman had wondered about this.

"And I'm Birdie. And this is my husband, the Captain."

Both girls stood silent and waiting, their eyes blinking like lighthouse lanterns. So was Captain his name then? He was dressed in a camouflage T-shirt with khaki combat shorts and black lace-up army boots. He looked every inch a captain.

The tall man brought his feet together, stamped one on the deck and saluted again.

The wooden deck shuddered. "I used to be in the army until my knee gave in," he barked, dropping his rigid gaze. It looked like he still held it against the knee.

"But once in the army always in the army, right, sweets?" added Birdie with a loving smile. He saluted his reply. She turned back to the girls. "Would you like a drink? I squeeze my own fresh carrot and cranberry juice. Oh, you must try some! Come on up to HQ. That stands for Headquarters. It's what we call our beach hut." She chuckled and quickly busied herself with tumblers and a jug of pale red juice from a cooler on the deck.

The girls climbed the deck stairs and stood there awkwardly, with their arms dangling. It didn't seem to matter that they didn't know what to say because Birdie loved to chatter. She told the girls about their daughter, Charlie, who was a little older than the girls. She told them that she liked to paint – watercolours of the ocean especially. It certainly made a change of pace from army life. Did they know that every year artists from all over came to Sunday Harbour especially to paint? It had something to do with the exceptional light.

The girls tried to look interested, but it was much more interesting looking around the beach hut. It was painted olive green and decorated with large maps tacked to the walls. There was a narrow army cot pressed up against one wall. A utility cupboard stood against another wall and useful items like a torch, a pair of binoculars, a compass, a brass bugle and a lantern dangled neatly from hooks.

Nicks was the first to notice the silence. Birdie had stopped talking and was staring at them expectantly, like she was waiting for a reply.

"Uh, oh, yes, definitely," guessed Nicks.

"That's what I thought," continued Birdie with a nod. "I told the Captain as much. Now," she tilted her head compassionately and smiled gently at the girls, "you must let us know if there's anything – anything at all – we can do for you."

Nicks nodded, smiling, and handed her empty tumbler back to Birdie. Coral stared down at her three-quarters-full tumbler of carrot and cranberry juice and turned to Birdie with pleading eyes. The juice tasted just like carrots and cranberries all mixed together (which wasn't particularly surprising, as Nicks pointed out later).

"Don't worry, dear, return the tumbler when you're finished."

Coral nodded gratefully and the two girls continued on to their hut. They'd bonded with the neighbours, and now they had to make a sign for the hut. How else would people find the Cupid Company head office?

They pulled the narrow double doors wide open and a puddle of yellow sunlight flooded the hut. The girls waded into its bright warmth and settled themselves in the middle, on the pink primrose rug. They had paper, coloured pens and each other. They also had carroty cranberry juice, but thankfully Romeo was enjoying that. That dog would eat or drink anything.

When they finally returned to the deck it was with a completed Cupid Company sign. Coral's mum was standing on the next-door deck, talking to Birdie. It looked like she'd been there for some time. The girls also noticed that she had three cans of paint at her feet. The women glanced up, saw the girls and waved. Coral and Nicks returned the wave but stayed put. They liked Birdie, but in a long-distance sort of way. They watched the little girl they'd called Shelly collecting shells on the beach instead.

It was five minutes more before Coral's mum finally lurched over with the paint tins. "I thought I'd never make it," she huffed.

"I know," agreed Coral. "Birdie does like to chatter."

Coral's mum narrowed her gaze and stared at her daughter. "I was referring to the paint tins," she finally replied. "They are heavy."

Coral knew that look; it meant she was bordering on a telling-off. "Well, thanks for the paint, Mum!" She grinned sweetly.

"Yes, thank you for the paint," added Nicks in her usual polite way.

"Shall we take a look?" But Coral was already examining the label on one of the tins. She inspected it with eyes that were wide with excitement, hoping that her dad had bought cerise pink; it really was her favourite shade of pink.

"Argh, no!" she suddenly cried out, like the beach hut had caught fire. "There's one tin of pale pink paint. The other colours are minty green and lemon pie!" She pulled a face, like she'd just actually been eating minty lemon pie.

"Really?" her mum said innocently.

"What are we supposed to do with these?"

"Well, the thing is, sweetheart," her mum began, choosing each word carefully, "they had a paint sale at Harry's Hardware. And you know your father... he got three tins for the price of one."

"But they're not even the same colour!"

"Well, that is true." There was no getting away from that fact. "But they only had the one pink tin left."

Coral's face pulled down with a frown while her mum took charge and opened the tins up one by one. "Take a look, the colours aren't that bad," she said, managing a very convincing smile.

Coral imagined the hut painted. In her head she pictured a hodge-podge, crazy-quilt sort of beach hut. Never mind the Cupid Company, once Coral Hut was painted it was going to look more like the Kooky Company!

Nicks had been staring at the multi-coloured paint tins too, but she was distracted by a bright red bow floating around elbow height.

"Is that your dog?"

It was the girl they'd called Shelly. One of her small hands pointed at Romeo, who was asleep in a deckchair; her other hand bulged with nut-coloured shells.

Coral liked little children; she even forgot about the mismatched paint tins for a moment. "Well, hello, Shelly!" she cooed. She would have liked a little sister.

"It's Ruby, not Shelly," the girl replied confidently.

Coral grinned. "Well, my dog's name is Romeo, Ruby."

"Can I stroke him?"

Coral nodded and the girl climbed the steps to the deck and stood quietly stroking Romeo, who raised one eyelid briefly but then found the effort too much. He continued snoozing while Ruby stroked his head between his ears.

"What are you girls doing?" Ruby finally

asked. Like all other small children her age, she was full of questions.

"We're going to paint our beach hut," explained Nicks patiently. "And we're trying to decide how best to use the colours we have."

Coral's grin disappeared with the sea breeze. "There is no *best* way," she grumbled. She then muttered something about pale pink, minty green and lemon pie and blew a raspberry.

"Do you know my big brother Jake?" wondered Ruby. "He goes to art college. He's very creative. Would you like him to help you paint your hut?"

The girls did not know a Jake and they both looked doubtful about his painting skills. He'd have to be very creative to solve their paint problem. But Ruby looked determined and gave Romeo one final pat – one that was firm enough to last him for a while. Romeo sat up, dazed.

"I'll go and fetch him for you. Bye!"

And then Ruby was gone, racing across the beach with her small heels kicking up a spray of sand.

the colour of love

Ruby was only gone a short while, although she was a lot slower coming back. They watched her small shape growing gradually bigger as she got closer. She had a tall blonde boy in tow, who looked a bit awkward. His hand was in her shell-free hand and she was practically dragging him along.

"This is my brother," she yelled out when she was still a few metres away. She continued pulling him along and only stopped when she'd finally reached the steps. "He's sixteen years old, and I'm six."

He was a handsome big brother. Big blue eyes definitely agreed with him.

Coral's mum emerged from inside the hut. "Oh, hello," she said, "I'm Coral's mum." The girls were still silent. "This is Coral. And this is Nicks."

The girls raised their hands and grew smiles between their bright pink cheeks.

"Look at the paint tins, Jake," ordered Ruby.

Nicks was the first to recover. "We need to paint our beach hut," she explained, "but these weren't... erm... exactly the colours we were expecting."

Suddenly Jake's awkwardness was gone. Being creative was obviously his thing. He bent at the waist and inspected the paint tins with a quiet 'mmm' sound. And then he stood up straight again. "Stripes!" he declared boldly. "Stripes in these colours will do very nicely. The hut will look bright and beachy."

The girls smiled. Suddenly the colours didn't seem quite so bad after all. And it had nothing to do with Jake's handsome face. Coral's mum loved the idea too and so she left them to it with a good-luck wave.

Jake passed out brushes and tins and gave the girls orders to paint every third wooden board with their particular colour. As they painted, Ruby cuddled Romeo or leaned over the railings and joined in their conversation.

It turned out that Jake and Ruby had only just moved to Sunday Harbour with their parents. They'd left their old friends behind and were looking forward to making new ones.

"Jake left his girlfriend behind too," Ruby added, and made a silent boo-hoo face behind her brother's back. She was all mischief.

Jake didn't respond, but his cheeks flashed like traffic lights.

"Her name was Victoria," Ruby continued shamelessly. "They even kissed."

It didn't seem possible for Jake's cheeks to turn any redder, but they did. "Ruby!" he rasped and sent her a scowl.

"Kissing is just kissing." She gave an innocent shrug of her shoulders, but seemed to sense that she was better off saying nothing more if she wanted to keep on her big brother's good side.

Coral was only half-listening; the thoughts stomping around her head were much louder than the voices in her ears. Jack had left his girlfriend behind. He knew almost nobody in Sunday Harbour... so he definitely needed the help of the Cupid Company to get over his heartbreak! Surely they could find him the perfect girlfriend? By the time they'd worked their way around to the front of the hut again, Coral had a firm plan in mind. She waited for her moment.

"Look at this!" she suddenly exclaimed (with oomph). "It's the Cupid Company sign!"

(She said 'Cupid Company' with a double dose of oomph). "I'll take it down so that I can finish painting, shall I?" She glanced sneakily at Jake. He continued to paint; he hadn't noticed a thing. But Coral would not be put off. "Yes, THE CUPID COMPANY – where we matchmake and help move true love along. I'll just rest the sign on this deckchair, the one right beside you, Jake." She was now speaking very loudly.

Nicks glanced over at her friend and frowned. Jake shrugged, but continued to paint.

'*What are you doing?*' Nicks mouthed silently to Coral.

'*Jake should be our first Cupid Company client,*' Coral mouthed silently back, and grinned.

'*How do you know he even wants a new girlfriend?*' Nicks looked doubtful.

Coral grimaced. '*Because he left his other girlf—*'

70

Jake spun round. "Are you girls OK?" he asked. The corners of his eyes were creased with suspicion.

Coral's mouth pulled wide and round as she made big O shapes with her lips. "Yes, thanks, Jake." She performed a few more stretched-O shapes. "I'm just doing my facial exercises. I do them often – especially when I paint."

"Do you paint often then?" he asked.

"Especially when I paint *and* when I'm at the beach hut. Also. Too..." The last few words faded from Coral's well-exercised lips. She wasn't making much sense.

It was time for Nicks to rescue her friend. She recognised the signs. She coughed and used her very best businesslike tone. "The Cupid Company," she explained thoughtfully, "finds people who are well-suited and matchmakes them." She then told Jake about their 'All for love and love for all' philosophy and even mentioned the questionnaires. She wanted to show him that they took their matchmaking very seriously indeed.

Jake looked sceptical. Ruby looked like Christmas had come early. "Oh, Jakey, it's just what you need!" she cheered. "If you get a new girlfriend then you won't miss Victoria so much."

"The Cupid Company is a great way to meet new people," added Nicks convincingly.

"So you've done this before then?" asked Jake, raising his eyebrows.

"Oh, yes!" joined in Coral. "We know exactly what we're doing. The last couple we introduced are actually still very much in love." She thought about Archie and Gwyn.

"Oh, come on, Jakey, please, please, please, please..." pleaded Ruby, like she might just cry for ever if he refused.

"Let's finish painting this beach hut and I'll think about it," he replied, a small frown growing between his eyes.

The girls – all three of them – clearly knew

when to keep quiet, and now seemed to be that time. And before long the front of the hut, the narrow double doors and the deck railings were also all painted with alternate pale pink, lemon and minty-green stripes. They stepped back to marvel at their handiwork. Even Romeo seemed to have forgotten about his game of seagull tag and paused mid-scamper to admire the glorious candy-striped hut. It looked fresh, fun and wonderfully beachy!

Jake inspected their handiwork with a satisfied grin. "Well done, girls, good job."

"Thanks, Jake!" Nicks and Coral chimed at once. Without his help the hut would never have looked this good.

"So would you like to sign up with the Cupid Company?" Coral blurted out. She couldn't wait a moment longer to find out.

Jake still looked doubtful.

"You have to – oh, please!" howled Ruby. She waited, reasons balanced on the edge of her tongue waiting to jump, just in case her brother said no.

Jake was silent for a while, but it was clearly rather difficult to avoid Ruby's desperate face. Finally he sighed. "Oh, OK then. But it's just a trial run – I can change my mind any time I like, right?"

Coral and Nicks nodded determinedly and hooked pinkie fingers. Their beach hut looked more beautiful than ever. And they had their first official Cupid Company client! Life seemed as bright and bouncy as a beach ball. Of course there was no way it could burst.

love letters

When the girls arrived at Coral Hut the next day they passed Birdie chatting with a lady with a baby who owned the beach hut two down from Headquarters. Birdie waved and the girls waved back. Romeo chased his tail in circles.

"Coral Hut looks wonderful," Birdie called out. Romeo chased even faster. Birdie laughed. "Romeo looks to be on top form too."

The girls grinned and climbed the pale pink, lemon and minty-green steps up to Coral Hut. Now that they had their first official client there was some serious work to be done. Nicks pulled out the deckchairs from their nesting place beneath the daybed and Coral unpacked a few essentials from her pink and purple heart-shaped backpack. There was Jake's completed questionnaire (that needed to be studied), two small cartons of fruit juice (not a carrot or cranberry in sight), sandwiches and half a packet of choccie biscuits.

"I'll fetch pens and paper," offered Nicks. She headed for the wicker basket and Coral reached for a biscuit to munch on while she looked out over the beach. A group of three old ladies stood waist-deep in the sea nattering to one another. They met every few days, and the old lady in the black swimsuit always wore a polka-dot shower cap over her hair. Coral munched another biscuit. Nicks did seem to be taking her time. Romeo sniffed the water's edge. He was probably looking for some seaweed to roll in. Finally Nicks reappeared. She glanced down at their stash of snacks.

"What happened to the biscuits?" she asked.

Coral shrugged innocently. She couldn't reply; her mouth was full. But Nicks seemed preoccupied with something else anyway.

"Look what I found," she exclaimed. She shook the papers between her fingers in the air, like her friend might recognise them. They just looked like a stack of envelopes to Coral. She tipped back her head (her mouth was still full of biscuit).

"They were in the wicker basket. We must have missed them before."

"What do they say?" Coral finally gurgled.

Nicks glanced down at the envelope on the top of the pile. "Every single one is addressed to Third Officer Perry Philips." She handed a few to Coral for inspection. "But they're all still sealed."

Both girls stared at the envelopes.

"Are they letters?" wondered Coral.

Nicks shrugged. "I didn't get that far. Shall we open a few?"

"Great-Aunt Coral did leave us the beach hut and all its contents," Coral hesitated. "I guess it would be OK."

They tore open the envelopes and took turns reading out loud from what did in fact turn out to be letters.

"*17 November, 1949. My dearest Perry, it seems cruel that we should be so far apart from one another with this cold, wide ocean separating us...*" read Nicks.

"*It feels like for ever since I last saw your face, but still your smile and your eyes remain bright in my heart and mind always...*" read Coral.

"*Every day I go about doing what I must do, but not a moment passes when I don't think of you, darling Perry...*"

78

"*I shall wait here patiently for you to return to me safe and sound, so please, my dear, be sure to take especial care of yourself...*"

"*Don't keep me waiting too long, although I shall wait without end...*"

Nicks paused reading and glanced up at her friend. Silvery tears slid down their cheeks.

"They're love letters!" they both cried out at once.

"And every one was written by Great-Aunt Coral, by the looks of things," added Nicks.

"To Perry Philips," finished Coral. She flipped a few envelopes on to their backs. "But where's his address? All each one says is the Royal Navy."

"And why were the letters never sent?" wondered Nicks. It was a mystery. "Maybe she didn't know where to find him. They didn't have the internet or email in those days, after all."

"Maybe he moved, and his letter to Great-Aunt Coral with his new address was lost in the post?" suggested Coral. They both gave this theory some quiet thought before Coral pushed on like a tug boat. "Or maybe he was a top spy and the Navy moved him to a secret location – one that Great-Aunt Coral could never ever know about? And there he met a Polish princess and she blinded him with money and cars and Jack Russell pups which helped him to forget about Great-Aunt Coral who in the meantime had spent all her time decorating this beach hut and reading her love poems thinking that he was being faithful and coming back but whoa-ho – little did she know. I've heard that some men are like that." Finally she ran out of story and imagination. Coral stared, wide-eyed and excited.

Nicks closed her eyes and sighed. "Well, either way, we really should return these letters to their rightful owner," she suggested sensibly. "I imagine Perry Philips is an old man by now."

Coral agreed with her friend. "I don't expect there's anything top secret about his location these days."

"Maybe my mum could help us track him down?"

"We could make it the Cupid Company's top priority," added Coral earnestly. Sitting side-saddle on her deckchair, she could easily peer inside Coral Hut. The cupids on the walls, the books of romantic poetry and now the forgotten love letters – at Coral Hut it really was *all for love and love for all*. The thought of doing something special for her great-aunt excited her too. She smiled a blissful sort of smile. Could this summer get any better?

Nicks promised to speak with her mum later that day; if anybody could find a telephone number or an address for Third Officer Philips it was her. With that settled, the next order of the Cupid Company business was Jake. They needed to find him the perfect girlfriend. How difficult could that be?

Nicks smoothed the creased questionnaire with her flat palm. Then she read out some of his handwritten replies.

"He was born in February. That makes him an Aquarius. His hobbies are anything to do with art – painting and sculpture especially, and sport. He loves sailing. He likes animals and Easter. He dislikes bossy people and eating cucumber. Under strange habits he lists doing quirky impressions of famous people."

Coral listened and then stared up at the clear blue summer sky for inspiration. "So he's a creative animal lover who likes sailing and pretends to be other people. Mmm."

They were both silent and thoughtful. Nicks stared at the very small pile of completed questionnaires pressed to her pink clipboard decorated with foil butterflies. It was barely even a pile. It was really only three questionnaires sitting one on top of the other. They'd all been posted under Coral Hut's door: one from Mr Gelatti, another from the Russian exchange student called Zinaida who worked part-time at the Seaside Store, and one from Miss Pane (even though they hadn't specifically asked her to). She was a dentist and best known for her root-canal treatments. She met lots of people through her job, but not many stayed longer than they needed to.

So this meant that they had questionnaires completed by a non-female, a non-English speaking person and a non-teenager. Not one was right for Jake. They would have to think harder to find the solution to this perfect-date dilemma.

"How about Delilah who works at the Sundog Art Gallery every school holiday?" suggested Nicks.

"She doesn't have the right hair for

sailing," replied Coral. "And Jake loves to sail." (Delilah had long, dark, very curly hair which she always wore loose so that it framed her head like a nun's veil. It was definitely the longest, curliest hair in Sunday Harbour.)

"Well, then, what about Paige Pockets?"

Coral thought about Paige for a few moments. She was a nice girl. And pretty too. But she always walked around with her shoulders hunched and her hands buried deep in her pockets, which was why they had nicknamed her Paige Pockets.

"She's quite a shy girl," Coral considered out loud. But then Jake hadn't seemed particularly talkative either. She imagined their first date in her head. It was very quiet. No, they had to find *the perfect* girl for Jake – somebody who was bubbly and could possibly introduce him to more new friends his age in Sunday Harbour. The reputation of the Cupid Company depended on it.

The girls sat in a puddle of silence. They

needed to find some way of getting more people signed up to the Cupid Company. And they both waited for the other one to come up with the bright-spark idea of how to do just that.

first love

The sea seemed to have a mind of its own. Some days it raced up and down the beach and skipped about to make waves; other days the water remained calm and clear. It was one of those days, and Romeo stood deep enough for his belly to get wet, catching fish – or trying to catch fish. He would spot one and dive for it, but he always went too deep and came up again, blinking the stinging salt from his small brown eyes.

Coral watched her pup from the beach hut deck. Romeo was much better at bobbing for bones. He'd even won first prize at the Lifeguard Charity Fundraiser the year before. Coral's lazy gaze slid from Romeo and continued down the beach. A grown man with a moustache, wearing dungarees and a black beret, was on his knees in the sand, concentrating on a small sand sculpture that looked like it might turn out to be the Statue of Liberty. A nearby mother worked hard at keeping her grabby toddler away from the growing statue. Further up the beach a tall girl with very long legs stood quietly and held the reins of a small brown and white chocolate pony.

"Is that Tabitha?" Coral called out to Nicks, who was trying to stick the Cupid Company sign to one of the hut's double doors.

"I wish that thing would stay up," Nicks moaned as she moved to stand beside Coral.

She followed Coral's pointing finger.

"Yes, that's Tabitha. She used to help my mum out at the post office, but that was before she started giving pony rides along the beach."

"Isn't she also in the school drama club?"

Nicks bounced her shoulders uncertainly. "I think she could be."

Coral rested both her elbows on the deck railing and gave the matter some thought. There was a small seed of an idea in her head; all that was needed for it to grow was a bit of quiet and some careful consideration. She tapped her chin thoughtfully. It didn't take too long.

"If they won't come to the Cupid Company, then the Cupid Company will come to them!" she suddenly cawed, showing all of her teeth to her best friend. At that moment she felt sure she'd been blessed with a streak of genius.

Nicks looked very confused, but it wasn't

the first time. So Coral explained.

"Jake loves sailing. Tabitha loves horse riding. So they're both sporty."

Nicks accepted this with a firm nod.

"And Jack wrote on his questionnaire that he likes animals. Horses are animals," Coral added brightly.

Nicks could have probably worked that last bit out for herself, but she nodded once more anyway. She was picking up the trail. "And Jake is an art student, while Tabitha likes the performing arts. So they're both creative."

"Do you think she could be the one for Jake?" Coral dared to ask.

They both tilted their heads and considered it for one careful moment. "Definitely!" they both shouted at once.

Suddenly there was the sound of barking. A frustrated Romeo was giving the slippery fish a good telling off.

But Coral wasn't out of ideas just yet. "The Lifeguard Charity Fundraiser is coming up," she continued. "Don't you think it would make the best first-date venue for Jake and Tabitha?"

Nicks ran the idea through her head. Every summer the beach came alive with sporty events like beach volleyball, the Sunday Harbour Great Swim, a search-and-rescue display and beach games (like bobbing for bones for pets) – all in the name of fundraising for the lifeguards. Everyone in Sunday Harbour looked forward to it.

"First we have to get Tabitha interested enough to sign up to the Cupid Company," replied the voice of reason.

Coral's nose wrinkled up. "Interested shminterested. Like who can resist the chance at true love? Come on, let's go and speak to Tabitha right away."

Coral believed that everyone was just like her; she thought that the entire world was in love with love. Nicks grabbed a questionnaire on her way out. She couldn't help herself.

They found Tabitha standing alone and feeding her pony oats from a small brown hessian sack. She looked up at the girls approaching. "Sorry – we're on a break," she called out to them. "You can come back in ten minutes though."

The girls drew up closer, but were careful to stay out of kicking or biting range (of the pony – the girl they trusted). They said their hellos and announced that they weren't after pony rides at the moment. Tabitha seemed to lose interest at that point. So Coral stepped in to jolly things along. She enthusiastically told Tabitha all about the freshly painted Coral Hut – perhaps she'd noticed the candy stripes while giving pony rides along the beach? But Tabitha stared blankly. So she moved on to the subject of the Cupid Company (where it was all for love and love for all) and how they were looking for the perfect match for the *very handsome* Jake. Tabitha still stared blankly.

"We believe you may be his perfect match," Coral spelled out.

"Who says I'm even looking for the perfect match?" asked Tabitha with a crinkle of suspicion criss-crossing her forehead. Some of the kids at school teased her for being horse mad. They even joked that she liked horses more than she liked people. Was that what this was about?

Coral's jaw dropped to the sand. *Like who wasn't looking for the perfect match?* Well, she wasn't. But she would be – one day.

"Jake is new to Sunday Harbour," explained Nicks. "He could do with making a new friend."

Tabitha considered this for a moment. She moved in a very small horsy circle.

"I'll do it!" she agreed with a grin. She turned to her pony and showed her teeth. Loyal to his owner, her pony suddenly raised his head, lifted his top lip and showed all of his teeth too. Tabitha laughed appreciatively.

Coral rolled her eyes at Nicks. Nicks was staring at the horse like it had just spoken. What other strange habits did Jake's future date have? But there was no time for second thoughts. Coral leaned forward, pulled the questionnaire from Nicks's fingers and passed it to Tabitha. "It's the Cupid Company policy – if you wouldn't mind just filling it in for us?" she asked politely.

Tabitha showed her teeth again and shoved the questionnaire in her back pocket with a firm nod. She would even drop it off at Coconut Hut personally.

Nicks handed her a business card and pointed to it, patiently explaining that it was actually *Coral* Hut, which was beach hut number five along the promenade. And then the girls left.

"Since when do you have business cards?" asked Coral as they made their way back to the beach hut.

"The *Cupid Company* has business cards,"

Nicks corrected her. "I just haven't given you your set yet."

"Oh, right." Coral thought about this. The idea of handing out business cards appealed to her very much indeed. She thought she might even personalise hers with her own name across the middle. *Coral of Coral Hut.* It did have a grand ring to it.

They returned to the hut to find Romeo asleep on the Cupid Company sign, which had fallen off the door on to the floor again. Coral was just shooing him off when Birdie appeared from next door.

"Hey-ho, girls," she called out merrily. The girls opened their mouths to reply but Birdie was too quick for them. She was instantly knee-deep in a monologue about Charlie.

"Charlotte is such a pretty name, and it was my great-grandmother's too, but what's the point because it's very girly and Charlie is not very girly at all. Anyhoo! She's home for the summer holidays – did I mention that she's a term boarder at an army school, even though the Captain took early retirement on account of his knee, but Charlie grew up in the army and once it's in your blood..." And then she suddenly stopped.

The girls stood there, silent and blinking.

"So what are you girls up to then?"

They were just about to answer when Birdie spied the soggy Cupid Company sign in Coral's hand. "And what's that? *The Cupid Company*," she read out loud. "What kind of a company is that then?"

Coral's eyes blinked one more time and then she came to life. She couldn't miss this business card opportunity. "Where are my cards, Nicks?" she hissed between clenched teeth.

Nicks pulled a business card from her pocket, about to hand it to their visitor, but Coral nimbly slipped it from her fingers.

"Here you go, take my business card," she said as she handed Birdie a small photocopied card with rough scissor edges. She then told her all about the Cupid Company and how their mission was *all for love and love for all*. Birdie listened closely. That was one thing about Birdie – she listened as well as she talked. And she only spoke when Coral had well and truly finished her Cupid Company broadcast.

"Oh, you must sign Charlie up to your Cupid Company!" she cried out. "That girl – dressed up in army khakis with big old boy pockets all over her big old boy trousers! Don't even get me started on the boots. And she's besotted with computer games. That X-Box thingamajig will send me senile. She needs to dress more like a girl and do girly things like meet boys and wear lip gloss. So you must put her on Cupid Company active duty alert. Can you do that?" She paused and pleaded with her eyes.

"She'll have to complete a questionnaire first," replied Nicks doubtfully. "And then of course we'll see what we can do." Her firm jaw and matching words hid the fact that she was starting to feel a teensy bit nervous. She had started to doubt their choice of girl for Jake, and now they had this girl called Charlie who dressed in 'big old boy pockets' to think about. It was quite obvious that Birdie was not going to forget about it. Matchmaking was beginning to look like it might not be quite the summer break they'd thought it would be, although it didn't seem like any of these thoughts had occurred to Coral. She was still smiling over her business card moment. How she'd enjoyed handing it over!

lovesick

Nicks held two pieces of paper in her hand. She passed one to Coral and left the other resting on her lap so that Romeo couldn't nip it from her grip. It was a new trick he'd learned. He'd worked out that grabbing things from people and then running away as fast as he could was the perfect way to start a game of chase. And it was one of his favourite games. Thanks to his Jack Russell ancestors,

98

he was a fast and nimble pup.

Coral stared at the paper in her hand. It was covered with numbers. She was not really a numbers sort of girl. "What's this?" she asked with a face that was miserable just in case.

"It's a list of phone numbers for all the Perry Philips my mum could find," replied Nicks. "I've already divided the list in two – and that's your half of the numbers."

"Oh, right." Coral's face brightened considerably. Phone numbers she could handle. The phone was actually one of her very favourite things.

"You need to work your way through the list and ask if any one of the Perry Philips at those numbers knew your great-aunt." Nicks spoke carefully. She watched her friend beam determinedly like she was up for the mission. She referred to the notes pinned to her foil butterfly clipboard and pushed on. "And the next order of business is Tabitha and Jake."

"Has Tabitha returned her completed questionnaire yet?" wondered Coral.

Nicks nodded and held up a questionnaire that looked like it may have spent the night in a stable. It had mysterious stains in different shades of brown along its edges and a large yellow greasy blot in the centre.

Coral pressed her nose closer to the mottled sheet of paper and sniffed. "Leather polish," she said, identifying one particular brown stain. She moved her nose along and sniffed some more. "Cheese spread." She kept sniffing until she reached the corner of the questionnaire. "And that," she gasped with screwed-up eyes, "is something very horsey..."

Nicks chuckled. "Well, Tabitha does love horses."

"And Jake loves animals," sang Coral with a go-get-'em grin.

"And according to this, Tabitha doesn't have any strange habits." Nicks tapped the empty lines in the questionnaire, which lay to the west of a stain that just might have been hoof oil.

Coral gazed out at her view of the beach and instantly sat upright. Her eyes were bright. "Well, I hope we've been good matchmakers, because here comes Jake now!" The possibility of true love excited her.

The girls watched Jake getting nearer. Of course Ruby was with him. She was wearing a shiny tiara in her hair, and as usual one of her small fists was full of hard brown shells she'd collected along the beach. Romeo recognised Ruby and raced up to her with his tail spinning like a propeller. He sniffed her hand and used his cold nose to prise her fingers open just wide enough to nip one of the shells between his teeth. And then he was off.

"Hey!" giggled Ruby as she chased after him.

"Don't go far," ordered Jake sternly before he turned to face the two broad smiles greeting him as Coral and Nicks leaned over the deck railings. He waved hello and buried his feet in the cooler sand which lay just beneath the sun-baked surface. "Could Ruby hang out with you for a while?" he asked. "My parents aren't far off, but she's bored and I'd like to go sailing."

Both Coral and Nicks nodded together. "Sure!"

This seemed like a good time to mention Tabitha. Coral seized the moment. "So, the Lifeguard Charity Fundraiser is almost here."

"It's the best day out ever," added Nicks.

"It's perfect for a first date."

"We've found you a lovely girl. She's called Tabitha."

"I would describe her as one of those girls who just has it all," Coral added with a dramatic roll of her eyes. "You know, I actually think she might have been Miss Sunday Harbour. Or if she wasn't she certainly should be! Ho ho."

Nicks stared straight-faced at her best friend. Her penetrating gaze said it all. *It was just like Coral to go too far.* "Yuh, so anyway," she interrupted before Coral got completely carried away, "shall we make it a Cupid Company date then?"

Jake had clearly heard about the Lifeguard Charity Fundraiser. He didn't know any Tabitha though. But then he didn't know many people in Sunday Harbour. And at least this girl would be about his age. "OK, fine," he finally agreed. He was obviously willing, but rather wary.

Nicks scribbled something on the back of one of her business cards. "Here's Tabitha's phone number – she's looking forward to your call."

She passed it to Jake with a polite, businesslike bob of her head. Coral glanced over enviously; she'd missed out on an opportunity to hand out a business card of her own. But that was OK; she was thinking of revamping her business cards anyway. Instead of simply 'Coral of Coral Hut', she was considering having 'Coral the Second of Coral Hut' on her business cards.

Suddenly Romeo returned, breathless, and threw himself in the shade of one of the deckchairs. A small shell dropped out of his mouth and he grinned victoriously. Ruby was only a few steps behind. She laughed and attempted to grab her shell, but it was slippery with doggy drool.

"You can keep that one," she cried out happily and plopped into the deckchair.

"Do you think that Coral the Second makes me sound like I'm second... you know, like *not first*?" Coral wondered out loud.

"That's what second usually means," was the reply. Nicks seemed preoccupied; she was staring out over the deck railings in the direction of Birdie and the Captain's hut.

"That's what I was worried about... Coral the Second has a fancy sort of ring to it... but second is not first…" Coral was deep in thought. Not that her friend was listening.

"Do you think that might be Birdie's daughter Charlie?" Nicks asked.

"Maybe I should just stick to calling myself 'Coral of Coral Hut'."

Nicks turned to face her chattering friend. "What are you on about?"

And then Coral noticed the girl on the deck of the khaki hut too. "Is that Charlie?" she asked.

They both stared closely. The girl looked a little older than them. Her hair was so dark it might have been black and it was pulled back in a neat, tight ponytail. Sure, she wore a T-shirt and sand-coloured cargo shorts that bulged with what could only be described as *big old boy pockets*. But she was really pretty too.

love hurts

In summertime the main beach of Sunday Harbour was usually a lively place, but every year on the day of the Lifeguard Charity Fundraiser the ground almost trembled with excitement and activity. The promenade transformed into a maze of wonderful stalls sheltered by multicoloured awnings. Food stalls sold hot dogs, pick-and-mix sweets, fresh fruit, pickled mussels served up in polystyrene tubs with toothpick forks, wrapped sandwiches, sticks of rock and giant lollipops. Other stalls sold curvy buffed-up shells, miniature brass anchors, straw sunhats, plastic sunglasses, blow-up beach balls, two-for-one sunscreens, beach fridge magnets, starfish mounted in wooden frames, driftwood art, buckets and spades and bright, thick towels.

The air was just as lively too. Mr Gelatti's ice-cream van played a loud, cheery tune. Seagulls squawked their interest. Small waves fizzed and frothed on the hot sand and all around people laughed, called out to one another and chatted eagerly. The girls had arrived in time to watch the thrill of the early morning set-up from their beach hut. Everyone was in a good mood; nobody seemed to mind the early start. And before long the rest of Sunday Harbour had arrived to enjoy the big day too.

First the girls and Romeo spent some time

with Nicks's mum; she liked the arts and crafts stalls especially, and they each came away with a pom-pom maker. You could make all sorts of things out of pom-poms, the stall-holder had promised.

They found Coral's parents taste-testing a selection of frozen yoghurts from a stall called the Frozen Cow. The girls didn't want to appear too interested in the frozen yoghurt out of loyalty to Mr Gelatti, who always gave them an extra scoop of ice-cream on the house (or van), but they agreed to a small taste of the peanut-brittle-flavoured yoghurt. It might have seemed rude not to. Romeo was less worried about this and licked his chops when a dollop of frozen yoghurt broke free and landed on the pavement between his paws.

A game of beach volleyball had started up and the girls moved over and settled into the sidelines to watch the Beach Boys versus the Mermaids. But they found it difficult to concentrate; they were too busy looking out for Jake and Tabitha. They just couldn't help themselves. The pair had to be somewhere! Not even the fact that cousin Archie and his girlfriend Gwyn were on opposing volleyball teams helped them to concentrate on the game. So they gave up halfway through and moved on to the start of the Sunday Harbour Great Swim instead. But they didn't bump into Jake and Tabitha there either. They did run into the Captain, Birdie and Charlie though.

"Hello, sweet-peas!" hollered Birdie the moment she set eyes on her beach-hut neighbours. "I have been on the lookout for you two. I can't wait for you to meet our lovely Charlie."

Charlie's face did not match the 'lovely' description at that moment. Her forehead was knotted up in a frown and her mouth was firm and straight. She was much more of a 'scowling Charlie'.

"Uh, hi, Charlie," the girls greeted her

109

nervously. Romeo sniffed her leather lace-up ankle boots suspiciously.

Charlie glanced down at the beloved pup. Coral was instantly fearful. But suddenly the dark cloud across Charlie's face lifted and a brilliant smile broke through. "Hello there, K-9," she said as she scratched his small, white, hairy head.

"Actually, it's Romeo," Coral corrected her.

"We call army dogs K-9s," explained Charlie with her smile still in place. "I guess it's just a habit." She shrugged like it was all very harmless.

Coral considered the new girl for a moment. Her hair was still scraped back in a tight, neat ponytail. Her T-shirt was the same dark colour and printed with the words *X-Box Mortal Kombat*. And she still wore cargo shorts with big old boy pockets, only this time they were a muddy olive-brown colour. She was definitely pretty though, and when she wasn't scowling, her eyes were kind.

"I really love what you're done with your hut – it's so colourful!" she said.

Both girls' eyebrows shot halfway up their foreheads. Charlie didn't look much like a pale pink, lemon and minty-green sort of girl.

"It is cheery," added the Captain, although it almost sounded like an order.

"And I've told Charlie all about the Cupid Company, haven't I, Charlie?" This came from Birdie, and she sounded firm too.

A small grey cloud returned to settle over Charlie's eyes. "Yes, you have, Mum." She sighed. She didn't look one bit like someone who wanted to be matchmade.

"Uh, we really should get going," squeaked Coral in a small voice.

"And Charlie, didn't I say that these lovely girls could possibly help you?" Birdie continued regardless.

"I don't need any help," said Charlie.

"So we're really looking forward to the start of the Sunday Harbour Great Swim,"

111

Coral mentioned brightly. Now would have been the perfect time for Romeo to chase a seagull.

"Didn't I say that they could find you a nice boyfriend?" persisted Birdie.

Charlie's shoulders slumped in defeat. "Yes, you did."

"That's settled then," decided Birdie, "Charlie will stop by Coral Hut first thing tomorrow morning if that suits you, girls?"

Coral and Nicks nodded like they'd actually had a choice. It seemed as though Charlie had no choice in the matter either. They all smiled weakly at one another and the girls waved goodbye to their military neighbours. *Until tomorrow* – they said with a smile. There was a lot of smiling. And then they turned in the direction of the sea. Suddenly there was Tabitha! And Jake was right beside her.

Coral and Nicks stood still, stuck on legs that wouldn't move. Their eyes were as big and round as lifebuoys. Tabitha was still dressed in jodhpurs. And she seemed to be nattering non-stop. She was providing demonstrations to her lively conversation too. There was Tabitha riding an imaginary horse over an imaginary jump. They watched Tabitha trotting on the spot with her head held high. Oh, and there she went, neighing and showing all of her teeth just like her pony had done that day on the beach. Jake was pale. He hadn't moved very much; he could only stare.

Suddenly a gun exploded and the Great Swim swimmers were off. The spectators spun in the direction of the water's edge, which had turned into a foamy wave of paddling arms and legs. The activity seemed to distract Tabitha, and for a moment Jake looked relieved. Everyone watched the swimmers head for the horizon, until finally they were nothing more than miniature arms and splashing feet.

The loudspeaker crackled and gave a

high-pitched screech. "Whoops, sorry, folks," boomed a very big voice. "Right, it's time for the beach games. And first up we have the pebble and spoon race. Would the entrants please line up between the yellow starters' flags. This will be followed by the piggyback race. Would entrants for this race please make their way over to the red flag."

Tabitha spun on the heel of her riding boot and put her nose to Jake's. She grabbed him by the shoulders and bounced up and down excitedly. Nicks and Coral watched her mouth moving rapidly; she was trying to convince Jake to join in a race. But was it the pebble and spoon race, or the piggyback race she was keen on?

Finally Tabitha's mouth stopped moving. She was obviously waiting for Jake's answer. His shoulders drooped and his chin landed on his chest. He didn't look like he wanted to enter either race. So Tabitha seemed to give his back a hearty slap to encourage him. And finally Jake gave a small, dismal nod of his head and the pair made their way over to the red flag. Tabitha leaped along joyfully; Jake's footsteps were long and heavy.

They joined the queue at the red flag and then finally it was time for the race to begin. Jake shuffled into place at the starting line, in between the yellow flags. Tabitha kept close to him and then pounced on to his back. Jack was not quite ready and he nearly toppled over backwards. Tabitha was a tall girl. But he recovered just in time and, following strict orders from his teammate, hooked his elbows behind Tabitha's knees. And then they were off.

Poor Jake staggered as fast as he could, but it was clearly not easy for him. Tabitha seemed to have confused him with a real horse and she writhed about, kicking him on with her heels and even slapping his rump a few times, just to get him moving faster. Coral and Nicks could hear her shouting from where they stood. 'Come on, come on!' Tabitha hollered with all the air in her lungs. But it wasn't enough. They were pipped to the winning post by two younger boys who were both light, wiry and as quick and nimble as Romeo. Jake seemed pleased to have the horrible ordeal over with, but Tabitha looked very unhappy. She shook her head and kicked the sand miserably.

Suddenly a silver streak shot across the golden beach. It was Ruby with her hair tied up in silver bobbles. Her arms were spread as wide as fishing nets as she ran to her big brother and landed an even bigger kiss on his cheek. Second place was just fine by Ruby.

love it or leave it

The Captain, Birdie and Charlie were early risers and had already settled into chairs on the deck of their beach hut by the time the girls finally found their way to Coral Hut the following morning. Birdie waved and hollered loudly: "Charlie will be over shortly!"

The girls waved politely and a dismal-looking Charlie sank deeper into her deckchair. But nobody argued. Birdie allowed them just enough time to fling open the narrow double doors of Coral Hut and haul out their own deckchairs before she nudged Charlie in the direction of the striped pale pink, lemon and minty-green hut. She arrived wearing a James Bond 007 T-shirt and looking almost shy. This changed when she caught a glimpse of Coral Hut close up.

She gasped out loud. "Your beach hut is just beautiful! Could I take a look inside?"

Both girls nodded and Charlie disappeared inside to marvel at the gold-framed cupids and the daybed overflowing with pillows covered in rambling roses, floral gingham and checks. She ooh'd at the pink primrose rug, she aah'd at the pretty stencilled white wooden floor. She even rubbed her cheek against one of the soft candy-striped throws for snuggling under.

Coral and Nicks were surprised by her reaction. With her James Bond T-shirt, severe ponytail and big old boy pockets, she just didn't seem like a pink-and-pretty girly sort of a girl.

Charlie returned to the deck and almost tripped over the Cupid Company sign, which had once again slipped off the door to the floor. She stooped to pick it up and glanced at it for a quick moment before handing it to Nicks.

"The Cupid Company..." she murmured out loud. "I guess it's time to get down to business then." She shrugged dully. She was clearly only signing up to make her mum happy.

Nicks made another attempt to reattach the now grubby Cupid Company sign while Coral rummaged through her back pocket. "Before we get started, you should have this," she announced as she handed Charlie a small white square of card.

Charlie read from it out loud. *"Coral of Coral Hut. Managing Director of the Cupid Company."* She glanced back up at the girls with a blank expression.

Coral grinned. It had taken her ages to write that on all her business cards, but it had been worth it.

Her grin was not lost on Nicks. "Since when are you Managing Director?" she demanded.

Coral shrugged like it hardly mattered and was really no big deal at all. "You can be Managing Director too if you like." But she said it in that way people sometimes do when they're trying to keep the peace.

"Why do we need a Managing Director in the first place?" Nicks wanted to know.

Coral made a face like this was the craziest question ever. "Why does McDonalds... why does Nike... why do any of these companies need a managing director!" She threw her arms around like a windmill.

"Uh, maybe because they earn millions and have like a million staff working for them?"

"And why do you think they earn millions and have millions of staff working for them?"

But Coral didn't wait for her answer. "Because they have top managing directors." It really was that obvious.

"So you'd make a better Managing Director than me, would you?" harrumphed Nicks.

"I already said that you can be one too," harrumphed Coral back.

"What's the point of a company with two managing directors, and like – nobody else?"

Charlie stood there with her arms hanging by her side and her head turning left then right with each comment like she was watching a game of tennis. Nobody spoke. Nicks glared at Coral. Coral glared at Nicks. Romeo snoozed on a deck chair and dreamed of gravy bones. And Charlie wondered why on earth she had been sent there. It looked like the Cupid Company needed more help than she did!

"I'll just be off then," she finally said. Her voice snapped the two other girls out of their glaring contest.

"Oh, no, please don't," pleaded Nicks.

"Yes, sorry about that," added Coral apologetically. They had not behaved very professionally at all.

"Please take a seat." Nicks gently ushered Charlie into the empty deckchair.

"And if you could just fill out this Cupid Company questionnaire," Coral said as she passed her a form with a pen. "We just want to know a bit more about you. Oh, and you'll notice that there are a few lines for any strange habits you might have," she quickly added as she pointed to the relevant section.

Charlie sent her a curious look. Coral replied with a *you-can-do-it!* grin and a supportive pat on the shoulders. So Charlie did her best to complete the questionnaire while the girls paced about and tried to look busy with other things when they really weren't very busy at all. And then finally Charlie stood up and glanced around like she had somewhere else to be.

"I'll wait to hear back from you then," she said as she delivered the questionnaire, which was now covered with blue scratchy writing. "But there really is no hurry at all," she added with a slightly nervous, twitchy sort of smile.

The girls watched her leave and Romeo stretched and yawned with his long pink tongue curled up like a fruit roll.

"Well, that went well," observed Coral.

Nicks could only manage a 'hmm' sound before she disappeared inside the hut to collect her foil butterfly clipboard. She returned to her deckchair and coughed to warm up her businesslike voice. "Right, now for the next order of Cupid Company business: have you phoned any of the names on your list yet?"

Coral thought about this for a moment and reviewed the previous day. She'd called the local radio station. She loved those phone-in competitions and had once even won free admission to the zoo for one whole year. She'd also phoned the local cinema to listen to the talking voice for the latest movie listings. She didn't like to miss a good movie, especially not if it was a love story. And she'd called *True Love* magazine to find out where the flower press she'd ordered (and paid for almost two weeks ago) had got to. 'Four weeks for delivery' seemed like a pointlessly long time to wait. But none of these things had been on a list.

"Which list was that again?" she asked carefully like there was still some chance she may have called the names on the list after all.

"Third Officer Perry Philips?" replied Nicks like she knew there was very little chance Coral had called the names on the list. "You forgot, didn't you?"

Coral shook her head passionately. Actually she hadn't forgotten. She now remembered exactly what had happened. She'd sat down to call the names on her list but then suddenly that competition had come on the radio. But she'd answered her question incorrectly (so

Brie was a French cheese and not the capital of France – her nerves had taken over), and because she'd felt low about losing out on the prize (a family trip to Paris – only the most romantic city ever!) she'd decided to phone the talking voice at the cinema. A movie could cheer her up. There was one showing with Daisy Duke.

This had reminded Coral about the overdue flower press. It had then taken her some time just to leave a message at the office of *True Love* magazine. And then, just as she had been about to get started on her list, her father had come marching through in his flannel pyjamas and towelling slippers and ordered her to get off the phone because money did not grow on trees.

Coral had read that in some really undeveloped countries they still bartered with things like bark and acorns, which did grow on trees, but felt that her father would not fully appreciate this worldly bit of news. So she'd slipped quietly off to her bedroom without managing to call a single telephone number on her list.

"Nope, I did not forget," she finally replied truthfully. "But my father had a wobbly about me using the telephone." It was essentially true. "But I'll phone every name on my list tonight, I promise." Nicks had a face like she didn't know whether to believe her friend or be annoyed with her. "I care about my great-aunt and Perry Philips too, you know," Coral added.

Nicks forgave her with a smile and Coral returned the smile, pleased to be on her friend's good side again. Nicks continued to smile so Coral continued to smile back. And then she realised that Nicks's smile reached way past her. Coral turned to see Ruby charging down the beach, kicking up her usual spray of sand behind her. She carried a large, flat square shape in one hand and a sort of dangly thing in the other. The girls didn't even notice Jake until the small girl arrived breathless at the bottom of Coral Hut's steps. Her hair was swept back with an Alice band decorated in fluffy white feathers. Her mouth was one big grin.

"Look what I've brought to show you!" she screeched happily, climbing the pale pink, lemon and minty-green deck steps.

Coral and Nicks had been keeping an eye on Jake, who was stomping along the beach after Ruby. He did not look particularly happy.

"What's that, sweetheart?" asked Coral as she dipped to Ruby's height. She was interested in what the little girl had to show them, but she was also very interested in avoiding eye contact with Jake – at least until they had *the perfect second date* lined up for him.

"This," gurgled Ruby with excitement, "is a painting my brother did." She held up a small stretched canvas decorated with a painting of a sailboat bobbing along the ocean at sunset.

It was beautiful. "And this," she continued after taking a deep breath, "is a garland string made out of shells I collected."

"You made this all on your own?" asked Coral, genuinely impressed.

Ruby nodded. "Well, mostly. Jake helped me to tie some of the knots in the string."

The boy who tied knots had just arrived at the beach hut. And he still didn't look any happier.

"Uh, hello, Jake," said Coral and Nicks with perfect timing. They both sounded slightly nervous too.

Jake made a sort of grunting sound that might have been a hello but then might not have been. He stood there, silent and brooding. "Is it OK if Ruby hangs out with you for a little while?" he finally asked. "I'm playing beach football – I'll be right over there." He pointed to a group of boys huddled around a ball just a short distance away.

The girls nodded and Nicks cleared her

throat. "We're sorry that your date didn't work out," she said kindly.

Jake's face crumpled like the memory was almost painful. But then, he *had* been raced like a horse.

"We will definitely do better next time," promised Coral.

"Next time?" Jake spluttered.

"Give us another chance," pleaded Nicks.

Ruby had been listening too. "Oh, please, Jakey!" she suddenly cried out. Jake stared helplessly at the three girls. He obviously felt pinned down by their big pleading eyes.

"All right then," he finally agreed with a sigh. He was a softie. "One more chance."

Pleading eyes quickly transformed into crinkly eyes and three girly grins. That was all true love needed – *one more chance!*

PUPPy love

Nicks arrived at Coral's house and plopped down on her bed beside Romeo, who was fast asleep on his back with all four paws sticking up in the air.

"Did you know," began Coral, "that two out of five people marry their first love? And that the world's oldest bride was 102 years old, and that red roses are the most popular flower to give on Valentine's Day?"

Nicks didn't seem particularly impressed. "No, I didn't," she admitted.

Coral closed the book she was reading and tapped its cover. "*Romance Trivia and Facts,*" she read out loud. "It's a useful book. I'm researching for my next school project."

"What school project?"

"I don't know – just the next one."

Nicks rubbed Romeo's up-down breathing belly. "So I called the rest of the Perry Philips on my list," she revealed. "But none of them knew your great-aunt." She looked disappointed.

"Well, then I should have better luck," replied Coral optimistically. "He's got to be out there somewhere. Come on."

The girls clambered off Coral's pink bed and headed for the phone. Romeo lifted one lazy eyelid and watched them leave. Would they return offering doggy treats and more belly rubs? It seemed unlikely, so he went back to sleep.

The straight-back chair with the tapestry cushion below the wall-mounted telephone had been replaced by a hard wooden stool. But Coral barely noticed. She perched on its cushion-free top and merrily dialled the number at the top of the list before asking – very politely – to speak to Third Officer Perry Philips.

The man on the phone replied that he worked on the railways and had never been to sea in his life.

So Coral tried the next number. An old man with a croaky voice answered.

But he'd never even known a person called Coral, let alone been in love with one.

A woman answered the third number on the list. She was Perri Philips – Perry with an i at the end. But she was very friendly, so Coral told her how they were trying to return some very old love letters to their rightful owner. The chatty woman thought this was a wonderful idea, so Coral also told her all about the Cupid Company and their motto 'All for love and love for all'. She also mentioned Coral Hut, the questionnaire and their success with Archie and Gwyn.

Perri thought it was the most romantic story ever.

Nicks frowned. At this rate they would never get through the list. She pinched Coral's bare toes. It took a bit more toe pinching, but finally Coral worked her way through every one of the phone numbers on her list but one. And that was simply because that particular Perry Philips was not answering the phone.

"We'll try again later," suggested Coral as she stood up and rubbed her aching bottom. That was the most uncomfortable stool ever. Her father would be pleased.

"It doesn't seem like our plan is working out," mumbled Nicks miserably. "I mean, what are the chances of Great-Aunt Coral's Perry Philips being the last one on our list?"

Coral shrugged as she headed back to her bedroom. "Stranger things have happened."

They found Romeo in exactly the same upside-down position, except he was now in such a deep sleep that his lifeless lips had been overtaken by gravity. His top row of small, white, pointy teeth were bared, rather like an upside-down growl.

Nicks slumped down beside the dog on the bed and pulled her foil butterfly clipboard and some pens out of her butterfly backpack.

"So what are we going to do about Jake?" she wondered as she got busy scribbling.

Coral cuddled up to Romeo and pulled his saggy top lip neatly over his teeth. But his lip just slipped down again the moment she let it go. "I'm not sure," she finally replied, "but somehow we have to find him the perfect date."

"The problem is we don't have enough people signed up to the Cupid Company yet."

Coral nodded her agreement. "That's true.

How can we matchmake if we have no one to matchmake with?"

Nicks's tongue crept up and over her top lip as she scribbled. "We should spend tomorrow handing out as many questionnaires as possible."

"I'd have to check with my mum first. Sunday is supposed to be family day." But of course Nicks knew that, and she nodded thoughtfully and continued scribbling. "What are you so busy with?" wondered Coral.

"My business cards." Nicks held one up in the air as proof. "See – *Nicks of Coral Hut. Joint Managing Director. The Cupid Company.*"

Coral was tempted to scowl, but then realised that she had no real claim to the scowl. Joint Managing Director had been her idea, after all (but since when had Nicks started listening to her ideas!).

"That's nice," she said simply instead.

There was a knock at the open bedroom door. It was Coral's mum.

"Hello, girls."

Romeo lay there. He remained motionless except for one eyelid, which snapped open. He stared at Coral's upside-down mum. He noticed her noticing him on the bed. He quickly snapped his eyelid shut again. And then he jumped up, landed on his paws and sprang from Coral's pink bed on to the doggy bed on the floor. It all happened so swiftly he was nothing more than a caramel and white streak across the room. He quickly snapped his eyes shut again and released a small, innocent snore from his nostrils.

Coral's mum frowned, but she decided not to say anything. She was in a very good mood. "Would you like to go on a picnic tomorrow?" she asked brightly.

"Where to?" wondered Coral because a picnic was, after all, about the location.

"There's a sailing regatta. And you know how hard your father works to organise these things." It wasn't really a question, but the girls nodded anyway. Coral's father was on the committee of the Sunday Harbour Sailing Club.

"Anyway, the club has a new member – a fellow who has just moved with his family to Sunday Harbour. We thought a picnic on the beach was a nice way to make them feel welcome. And it'll be fun to watch the boats. You're welcome to join us, Nicks."

The girls turned to each other and had a silent conversation. They'd been best friends for long enough to be able to do this.

Sailing regatta = busy beach.

Busy beach = lots of people to give Cupid Company questionnaires.

Brilliant!

They both turned to Coral's mum and grinned. "We'd love to!" they cried out.

Coral's mum was vaguely surprised by their enthusiasm. Family days out were not always met with quite this much gusto. "Oh, good," she replied as she made for the door.

Romeo had been sneaking a peek through the slits in his eyes, and Coral's mum turned and gave him a parting glare. They seemed to be having their own little silent conversation too.

Don't think you have me fooled, Romeo.

Zzz.

And don't even think about climbing back up on that bed!

Zzzzzzz.

tough love

Coral's mum packed the best picnics. There
was a hamper full of food and chilled drinks
and a big blue-checked blanket, all ready for
the arrival of the sailing club's newest
member and his family. Coral's father helped
to unpack the food. First he unpacked
frankfurters with a label that read TWO FOR
THE PRICE OF ONE on the wrapping. He
looked pleased. And his smile grew even

wider when he came across a box of sesame breadsticks dressed in a HALF-PRICE sticker.

"Well done!" He showed Coral's mum a thumbs-up. She rolled her eyes at the bright blue sky above and contemplated a sigh while Romeo, who was at the water's edge, suddenly started barking crossly. A small frothy wave had washed over his paws.

"Can we go and see the boats?" asked Coral.

Both her parents glanced up at the boats that were bobbing along the water or beached on the sand. "Yes, but don't go too far," advised her father. "Our new friends will be here soon."

So with a pile of questionnaires pinned to Nicks's foil butterfly clipboard, and a wad of business cards in each of their pockets, the girls set off. They really did want to see the boats too. Some were new and shiny; others were older and dull with tide marks traced across their hulls. There were boats with colourful canvas sails and boats with plain sun-bleached sails. Some had names like *Wind Chaser* and *Wave Dancer*; some just used numbers to identify them. The girls walked along the hard wet sand, and then saw a face they recognised. Actually, it was two faces. One face belonged to Jake, the other to Ruby, who had her hair in pigtails bound with electric-blue fake-furry scrunchies. They both wore bright yellow life jackets and were very busy wiping down a tiny washed-out boat that had a very small faded number painted on its belly.

Ruby noticed the girls and raced over with a cloth in her hand. "Come and look at our boat!" she screeched excitedly.

They couldn't refuse, and arrived wearing slightly nervous smiles. They were still no closer to finding Jake the perfect date and hoped he wouldn't ask.

"Your boat is really nice," observed Nicks, who was always sensible in stressful situations.

"It's not my boat," replied Jake. "And it's kind of old, but it'll be fun to sail. We're entering the obstacle course."

"The obstacle course is much more about skill than speed," recited Ruby like she'd heard it said many times before by somebody else. "And I'm going to be co-pilot."

"Can you really sail boats?" Coral was astonished.

Jake smiled at his small sister. "You only really need one person to sail this boat, but you've got to have a two-person crew to enter the competition."

"And Jake is the best sailor in the world," added Ruby. "Our race is at twelve o'clock. You must cheer us on!"

The girls smiled enthusiastically. It was the least they could do after the Lifeguard Charity Fundraiser piggyback-race shambles.

"Of course we will. And good luck!" they called out heartily as they arced their way back in the direction of the picnic hamper and blue-checked blanket. Coral's father had said not to go too far. But there was still time to hand out a few Cupid Company questionnaires.

They bumped into Mervin, who rented out umbrellas from a hut on the beach every summer. They also met up with Pippa, who delivered pizzas on the back of her Vespa scooter. Jade, who lived two doors down from Nicks, was with a friend, and they both agreed to complete a questionnaire. And only then did the girls head back to the picnic for a drink. It might have been the hottest summer's day ever, and they almost melted onto the blanket.

"Well, hello there!" boomed a voice from above.

They all looked up and squinted into the bright white sunlight. There was the outline of a tall man, a lady and a girl standing over them. Romeo wagged his tail just in case the newcomers had brought treats.

"Lovely to see you," replied Coral's father

as he stood up and shook the man's hand. They all quickly found their feet and introduced themselves one by one. Coral's father's new friend was called Eddie. His wife was called Mary. And the young girl was called Lexie which, they were told, was short for Alexandra. She was a little older than Coral and Nicks, and very pretty. She smiled and her pink cheeks dented with two dimples.

"So do you like Sunday Harbour?" asked Coral politely.

Lexie smiled and nodded. "It's different, but nice. We used to live in a big town. But I do like boats. Hey, is that your dog?"

Romeo was standing up on his two hind legs and trying to look as cute as he knew how. He'd spotted the two-for-the-price-of-one frankfurters and hoped that somebody might give him at least two.

"That's Romeo." Coral patted his head lovingly. "And yes, he's my pup."

Lexie knelt down and gave his belly a good rub. "He's cute."

Romeo seemed to think that Lexie was cute too, and he licked her cheek. She giggled. She didn't appear to mind the doggy drool one bit and was so busy playing with Romeo she seemed to forget about the girls for a moment, which was just as well. Coral had just had a flashbulb moment. She was overcome by a genius idea.

"Nicks!" she hissed and gestured her friend a short distance away from the picnic blanket. "She's perfect!"

Nicks frowned. "Uh, I guess she is a nice girl."

"What I mean is – she's perfect for Jake."

"You've just met her!"

"Sssh, keep your voice down. I know enough – like she's also new to Sunday Harbour. And she likes animals and boats."

Nicks wasn't convinced. They'd messed up once already. There seemed to be a bit more to the business of romance than they'd first thought. But then again, new-girl Lexie might also like to make friends in Sunday Harbour.

"All right then, we'll hand her a questionnaire later," she finally agreed.

Coral was preoccupied. "There's no time for questionnaires. Today is the perfect day."

"For what?"

"For the perfect date!"

"But we really don't know enough about her yet."

"She can take the questionnaire verbally," declared Coral impulsively before charging back in the direction of Lexie and Romeo.

Nicks scrambled after her but it was too late. Coral's arms were crossed and her forehead was crumpled in concentration as she paced. "So tell me, Lexie," she began like a lawyer at a trial, "do you like all animals or just dogs?"

Lexie laughed as Romeo nipped playfully

at her blonde curls. "Oh, I love all animals."

Coral paused her pacing and showed Nicks a secretive thumbs-up. "Right. And do you have any creative hobbies?"

Lexie paused to think about this. "Well, I make jewellery, I guess that's creative. This is my favourite bracelet I made." She held up her wrist and showed off a string of frosted glass beads in bright colours that glinted in the sunlight. It was very pretty.

"That is creative," nodded Coral appreciatively. "And if we could just go back to this business of boats. You say you love them. How much do you love sailboats?"

Lexie made a face like she was starting to find the questions slightly strange, and Nicks tipped her eyes at the heavens. But Coral was not put off. She tapped her fingers thoughtfully while she waited for her answer.

"Well, I've never actually been sailing, but I know I'd like to. It's one of the reasons why my father joined the sailing club."

Coral waited to see if Lexie would add anything further, and then nodded like her reply was satisfactory. "Yes, that is good. And finally, do you have any strange habits?"

Lexie turned to her with a very confused expression. "Strange habits?"

"Yes, you know – things that are not entirely normal. For example, Nicks over here practises silent kung fu when she concentrates and also sleeps with the bedcovers over her head."

Nicks's cheeks caught fire. She would have replied with a list of Coral's strange habits, but then they'd surely be there all day! She said all this with her eyes though as she glared at her best friend.

Lexie stammered. "Well, I suppose I do. I guess." She thought for a moment. "I do have to peel the labels off bottles before I can drink from them. And I read magazines back to front," she suggested, almost hopefully, although she really wasn't enjoying this game

148

of get-to-know-you any more.

Coral nodded. These seemed to be perfectly acceptable strange habits. She then thought back to Jake's questionnaire. "And for my final question, Lexie. Are you a particularly bossy person, and do you like cucumber?" (Jake wasn't fond of either of these things.)

Lexie looked more confused than ever, but she finally shook her head. "I'm not bossy," she cried out. "And I prefer not to eat cucumber if I can help it."

"That'll do, thank you," concluded Coral. She grinned broadly at her friend. They had a winner! "Mum, I'll be back in a minute. I need to have a word with Ruby." And then she was gone.

the love boat

"Do you girls want a snack or will you last until lunch?" asked Coral's mum as she passed fruit and biscuits out to her picnic guests.

"Actually, we thought we might take a closer look at the boats," replied Coral eagerly. "Lexie loves boats."

Lexie smiled warily and nodded, even though she wasn't so sure she did love boats any more. This Coral girl was making her nervous.

"I promised to stop by the sailing club's organisers' tent," added Coral's father. "Perhaps Eddie would like to meet a few more club members?"

Lexie's father nodded eagerly. And so off they all went, with Lexie wedged safely in between her father and Nicks.

They soon came to Jake and Ruby's boat, which was still beached on the sand even though it wasn't long before the start of their race. Jake waved an unhappy hello and Ruby looked across at Coral to give her the nod, then she clutched her tummy.

"What's wrong?" asked Nicks quickly.

Ruby pressed her hands against her belly and screwed her face up tight. "I... think... I... ate... something... bad!" she said slowly and rather loud.

Nicks patted the small girl's shoulder. "Oh, you poor thing."

Ruby relaxed her face to take a small peek at her audience and then crumpled her eyes up even tighter. "Yes, it hurts so much! I don't think I can take part in the race." She made a small 'boo-hoo' sound and once again checked her audience through the slits in her eyes. Jake looked distressed.

"We should take her to the lifeguard's station," suggested Coral's father firmly.

"Don't worry about me, I'll live!" Ruby cried out with her hand pressed to her forehead.

Coral was very impressed. Ruby reminded her so much of herself when she was that age.

Ruby clutched her tummy again. "We must find Jake a new sailing partner."

Now Nicks was in on what was going on. And she was not in the least bit surprised. Lexie, on the other hand, hadn't clicked at all, and was now convinced that life by the sea did strange things to your brain.

"Well, I'm no good in boats," said Coral, with wiggly eyebrows directed at Nicks.

Nicks sighed. What choice did she have? "Me neither," she joined in half-heartedly. This was not how she would have done it.

"And the fathers are too big for this boat," added Coral. "Hey, Lexie – you said you love boats." She put on her brainwave face.

"But I've never sailed before."

"All you have to do is sit there!" Ruby cheered and then quickly clutched her stomach again.

Jake just wanted to enter the race. "I have my sailing badge," he mentioned. "We don't go out very far and we do wear lifejackets."

"It's all very safe and well organised," agreed Coral's father, who prided himself on the sailing club's very high standards.

Lexie's father seemed to be taking this all in. He looked at Lexie questioningly. It really was up to her.

Lexie stared back at all the faces staring at her. She had said that she liked boats. And just sitting there couldn't be that hard. "All right... fine," she said, in a voice that was smaller than usual.

Jake grinned gratefully and passed her a lifejacket. They didn't have very long, and he clearly wanted to outline the very basics of what would happen once they were out on the water to her. He was a sailor who liked to be prepared.

Coral, Nicks, Coral's father and Lexie's dad returned to the picnic to watch the race. They were on a slight rise and had a very good view, especially since the boats would be sailing in line with the shore. They watched carefully as the little sailboat tacked out and joined the other boats streaming through the starting buoys. Then the claxon sounded and they were off, heading for the first set of red buoys which the sailboats were required to weave through.

Jake was at the back of the boat with his hand firmly gripping the rudder to steer the boat. Lexie was perched near the front of the boat and holding on very tightly. At first glance she appeared to be doing fine; it was only close-up that the faint shade of green that was starting to colour her face became noticeable.

It came time for Jake to loosen the sails, and he reached over to the boom and pulled on a rope. It released the sail with a 'whoosh' noise. Lexie yelped loudly and jumped. The sound of her yelp caught Jake by surprise and he almost dropped the rope in his hand.

He returned to the rudder and asked Lexie if she was OK. She nodded but didn't speak. She just kept her head straight and turned quietly greener. A boat pulled up alongside them and its passenger waved and called out merrily. Lexie leaped in the air and shrieked once again. Anything loud or unexpected always gave her a fright.

Jake nearly lost his grip on the rudder – he clearly wasn't used to screeching girls. But he finally made it through the red buoys. Boats

155

passed him. His borrowed boat was probably the oldest one there that day. And his co-pilot's spur-of-the-moment sound effects weren't helping either.

The audience on the shore was too busy cheering the two sailors in the small boat on to notice exactly what was going on. Lexie, meanwhile, had turned even greener.

They reached the end of the first lap. It was now time for Jake to turn the boat around and go back the way they had come. He revisited the boom to tighten the sails, only this time he warned Lexie before he did anything. She nodded and took a deep gulp of salty air. And only then did she speak.

"Jake, I don't feel very well. I think I might have what Ruby has."

Jake thought about this for a moment and grunted. "You're probably seasick." It was normal for a first-time sailor. "Try to breathe deep and focus on the horizon."

Lexie did as she was told while Jake

struggled to tighten the sails. But it wasn't enough to save the day.

"I'm sorry, Jake!" she cried out miserably, just moments before she was very sick all over the small deck of the nameless sailboat. Jake grabbed on to the dangling rope just in time to avoid skidding overboard.

Coral stared from her perch on the blue-checked picnic blanket. Her shoulders slumped. They'd all seen exactly what had happened. It was probably the second-to-worst date in history. Nicks knew it too. Even Ruby understood that things had not gone quite as planned (so it was just as well that they were the only three there that day who knew that it was actually a date in the first place). Nicks glanced over at Coral and sighed. This was exactly why *she* should have been Managing Director of the Cupid Company.

love lost

Having their own beach hut meant that the girls had to take care of it too. Coral's mum had been careful to make this very clear. That meant tidying and dusting and sweeping the sand from the floor at least once a week. That was the worst job; the beach seemed determined to find its way inside. So the girls took turns. Coral usually complained while she swept, but this time she hummed a quiet tune. It was better to keep a low profile – at least until her best friend had stopped scowling at her, anyway.

"Every decision should be a joint one," continued Nicks as she dusted the book shelves. "And if you'd have asked me, I'd have said that I thought the sailing date was a very bad idea."

There was a lot of sand in the hut that day and Coral was entertaining happy thoughts of vacuum cleaners.

"Are you humming?" demanded Nicks.

Coral glanced up at her friend. She sensed a question hanging in the atmosphere. "What?"

Nicks sighed and continued dusting. "You weren't even listening to me, were you?"

"Of course I was! And yes, I did phone the final Perry Philips on my list. And no, he didn't know Great-Aunt Coral. So what do we do now?"

Nicks paused with her duster and studied

the air for answers. "We must write to the Royal Navy and ask them for any information they have on Third Officer Perry Philips."

"What a fabulous idea, Nicks!" Coral cheered a little louder than she would normally have done.

Nicks's straight mouth curved slightly in the corners. She never could stay annoyed with Coral for too long. "I'm done here. You finish up sweeping while I get a pen and writing paper."

Half-heartedly Coral picked up the broom she'd dropped to the floor, even though she felt that the letter should take priority over sweeping. But she moved double-time and finally joined her friend and Romeo outside. The pup was laying belly-down with his front paws and chin hanging over the edge of the deck. He was studying the sand below for crawling crabs.

Nicks had almost finished the letter already. She read out what she'd written and then looked up at Coral for her approval.

It was a good letter. It said everything it needed to say. Well, almost. "We should end the letter by signing it from Coral and Nicks, Managing Directors of the Cupid Company. And below that we could add 'All for love and love for all'. Every opportunity is an advertising opportunity," Coral added professionally.

Nicks stared at her blankly. "No."

"No to which bit?"

"No to all of that except for signing it from Nicks and Coral."

"Or Coral and Nicks. You know, like uh, either way..." The laser-beam look from Nicks dissolved the end of her sentence.

Suddenly Romeo barked. And then Birdie appeared at the top of the deck stairs. Charlie followed closely behind her, but obviously not closely enough.

"Come on, Charlie," urged Birdie. "Hi, girls! How are things going over at the Cupid Company head office?"

"Definitely very good," replied Coral with all the enthusiasm she could find inside her. "We almost have a shortlist of perfect dates for Charlie." She did say 'almost'.

Birdie did look pleased (Charlie less so). "That is exciting! We can't wait, can we, Charlie?"

Charlie stared blankly ahead. "Nope, we can't wait," she said in a voice that was as flat and heavy as an anchor. Thoughts of going on a date seemed to be dragging her down.

"So when do you think Charlie will go on her first date?" wondered Birdie eagerly, Charlie clearly cringing.

Coral hid her hands inside her pockets and fiddled with a hard wodge of dried tissue that had gone through the washing machine.

"Oh, soon. Very very soon," she replied while she rocked on her heels. She didn't like making it up as she went along, but what else could she do? There was pressure from every side. Jake would probably never date again thanks to them. And now they had to find a date for Charlie: a girl who liked computer games, the army and wearing trousers with 'big old boy pockets'. At that moment the Cupid Company felt more like the Stupid Company! Would they ever get it right?

But Birdie knew none of this. "Alrighty, girls," she sang, "we'd better be off. We're going shopping. Charlie is thinking about buying a few skirts." She looked to Charlie for confirmation of this. Charlie nodded very slowly. Yes, that had been her answer: she'd *think* about it.

They waved goodbye and the girls slithered into their deckchairs. Nicks still had their letter to the Royal Navy in her hand. She waved it in the air gloomily.

"Well, at least we're one step closer to bringing Great-Aunt Coral and Perry Philips together again. My mum will post this for us."

For a while Coral was silent and thoughtful. And then she suddenly sat up straight, grinned and shouted out: "I know exactly what we should do!"

Nicks looked pleased. This was very good news, because she was all out of fresh ideas.

"We should have a party!"

Nicks's grin deflated until there was nothing left of it. "How will a party solve our problems?"

"It might not solve all our problems, but it will cheer us up."

It was just like Coral to think about having fun when there was work to be done. Nicks frowned. But then Coral was very good at having fun. And she always made other people smile. Just thinking about it made Nicks smile. Maybe a party was just what they needed after all.

love conquers all

Ruby was fizzing with excitement. Parties were her favourite thing, and she arrived at Coral Hut with a bag full of brown, cream, pink and pearly silver shells. Some were quite big, while others were small and dainty, and each one had been hand-collected by Ruby herself. Coral and Nicks picked a few up and admired them with 'oohs' and 'aahs'.

"I'm going to make garland strings of

shells to decorate your hut with," Ruby revealed proudly. "And I brought these with me too. Jake made them and said we could hang them as decorations for the party." She held up a smooth piece of driftwood shaped like a sliver of the moon. Rows of pretty shells hanging from fishing line dangled from the driftwood like wind chimes. There were three more just like it, although the driftwood was a different shape with each one. Romeo sniffed at the musical creations, unimpressed, and then wandered off to snooze beneath a deckchair.

"They are beautiful!" breathed Nicks.

"Coral Hut is going to look very special," added Coral with bright eyes.

"What have you girls been doing?" asked Ruby. The hut's deck was scattered with pens and paper and a small wad of notepapers weighed down with a lump of washed-up coral.

"Those are our party invitations." Nicks

picked one up and handed it to Ruby. "Here you go. It would be nice if Jake came too."

"I don't think Jake will come," admitted Ruby.

"But why not?"

"He says things get weird whenever you two are around."

"But we're going to play beach games," added Coral, like it might change things.

Ruby just shrugged and rattled her bag of shells. "I'm just telling you what he says."

So Nicks scooped up the driftwood wind chimes and got busy hanging them from the deck roof. Coral helped her, but nobody spoke for a while. They were all very busy with their own thoughts.

One pink, one pearly, counted Ruby in her head as she threaded the shells.

Things only get weird when Coral is around, sulked Nicks.

I wonder if I should dress Romeo up as Cupid for the party? contemplated Coral. *I*

could attach little wings to his back—

"Hi there," came a voice. That was the end of the girls' quiet thinking, and they all turned towards the sound. It was Charlie standing at the top of the deck stairs.

"Hiya," they replied at once.

"I need to get away from the skirt talk," Charlie grumbled with a scowl. "Mind if I hang about here for a while?"

The girls shook their heads and Charlie watched, mesmerised, while Nicks hung another wind chime. She appeared to be captivated. "They are so beautiful," she whispered.

"Ruby's brother Jake made them."

Charlie moved closer and ran her hand across the dangling shells that swayed in the cool sea breeze. "He must be very clever. I don't think I've ever seen anything quite so pretty. I'm not very creative at all."

"We're decorating the hut for a party," revealed Coral as she handed Charlie an invitation. "Please come!"

Charlie stared at the small square of card and sniffed it. The scent of the paper made her smile. Just because she liked computer games and trousers with big old boy pockets didn't mean that she didn't like to look at pretty things too. After all, she'd loved the hut when she'd first seen it and what could be more girly than that?

"I'd love to come to your party," she finally replied.

"I'm making garland strings to decorate the hut with," said Ruby proudly.

"They're pretty too," admired Charlie, but she couldn't seem to drag her eyes away from the driftwood wind chimes for very long. Her eyes twinkled as the shells made soft delicate clunking sounds and gleamed in the warm sunlight. They really were exceptionally lovely.

"Charlie!"

They all turned to the voice.

"It's time to leave the unit. Fall into formation."

It was the Captain, and he was waving Charlie over with stiff arms.

Charlie groaned and rolled her eyes. "It's time for a beach run and press-ups."

"Sounds like fun." Coral smiled. It didn't sound like fun at all, but she didn't want to make Charlie feel bad.

"Hardly! I make a much better couch potato. But I like hanging out with the Captain." Charlie grinned, gave a firm salute and then raced across the sand.

The girls watched her leave. Only Coral stared a bit longer than usual, but it would have taken somebody standing really close by to notice that her eyes had glazed over. She was preoccupied with the thoughts inside her head.

"So she doesn't like sports," she mumbled as she stared. "She's not the creative type either..." She glanced from Nicks to Ruby and back to Nicks and then finally released her thoughts into the open air. "I think Charlie is the one!"

Nicks especially looked confused. "The one for what?" Ruby simply continued stringing shells.

"The perfect one for Jake! I think I know where we've been going wrong."

Ruby looked up from her shells; Nicks looked apprehensive.

"We've been looking for somebody who likes all the same things Jake likes. But everybody is different – and that's what makes it fun. Charlie isn't like Jake at all. But maybe that means they'll like each other even more!"

"Opposites attract," agreed Ruby with a careless shrug. *Everyone knew that*, she thought to herself as she focused on stringing the next shell. "But Jake still won't come to your party."

Coral stared intensely. The cogs and wheels of her brain were turning so fast they were smoking. And then she smiled a very slow, mischievous smile.

"We'll see about that. When it comes to all for love and love for all, the Cupid Company does not give up easily!" She was now standing tall with her shoulders back and her feet spread wide apart like an all-powerful superhero. For one brief moment, she was Captain Clever.

Nicks had seen this look in her friend's eye before, more than once. She knew exactly what it meant too. It meant that something weird was about to happen. Again.

love to bits

"I really don't see how this is going to work," Nicks groaned.

"Keep writing," ordered Coral. "And I already told you, it's the perfect idea."

Nicks felt that the words 'perfect' and 'idea' should never be used by Coral in the same sentence, but she sighed quietly and did as she was told. She continued writing at the bottom of each and every party invitation:

BRING A STUFFED TOY ALONG AND HELP SUPPORT THE SUNDAY HARBOUR SAILING CLUB'S *TOYS FOR AFRICA* CAUSE.

Of course Coral had cleared it with her father first. And of course *Toys for Africa* was a very worthy cause (some of the poorest children in Africa had never owned a toy of their own). But it didn't hurt that as a member of the sailing club, Jake would feel duty-bound to attend their party. It was a very smart plan.

Coral grinned smugly and stared across the beach. Just metres from the water's edge a young man with bulgy muscles wearing stretchy shorts lifted hand weights over his head – one up, one down, up, down. He concentrated on the horizon while he counted the ups and downs. Not far away an older man lay lifeless on a lounger with a handkerchief spread across his face. It fluttered up and down with every breath the snoozing man took. And in between them a seagull picked at the crusts of a sandwich a forgetful fisherman had left behind.

Coral thought about Charlie while she stared ahead. Should they tell her about Jake? It was always good to be prepared. But would it make her too nervous? Mmm. She felt a tug on her shoelaces and found Romeo staring up at her with his puppy eyes. He had a red ball covered in drool between his paws. He wanted to play catch.

So she scratched his head and tossed the ball over the deck railings. But her fingers slipped on the drool and the ball flew west instead of east. It sailed in the direction of the snoozing old man and collided with his fluttering handkerchief. But the ball didn't stop there, and continued floating through the air with the handkerchief for a sail. It finally landed in the sand a few metres away with a faint plop.

The old man sat upright and squinted into the sunlight. He waited a moment for his eyes to adjust to the bright light and then glanced around him for his missing handkerchief. But he didn't search far enough. How did handkerchiefs simply disappear? He seemed very confused indeed.

Romeo was just as confused. He was looking for a red ball, not a handkerchief. He ran around in circles and bobbed his head this way and that. He'd never known a ball to simply disappear before. Well, there was that one time, but he was quite sure the sneaky waves had been responsible for that magic act. He knew never to trust the waves.

Coral was about to solve the riddle for the dog and the old man when suddenly her mum appeared at the top of the deck steps. She was smiling.

"Girls – I have a surprise for you!"

Coral instantly forgot all about the red ball caught up in the handkerchief. Surprises were one of her favourite things.

"Considering that you're collecting toys on

behalf of the sailing club's *Toys for Africa* cause, they have decided to allocate you a small party fund for drinks and snacks. And I'd be happy to arrange it all for you. In fact, I already have some super-beachy ideas." Coral's mum rubbed her hands together gleefully. She was the queen of snacks (a talent which was not limited to picnics).

Coral turned to Nicks who turned to Coral. They grinned.

"BRILLIANT!" they crowed.

Coral's mum smiled. "How about blue jelly set with gummy fishes that look like they're swimming about? And fish-shaped crackers, sandwiches shaped like starfish and chocolate chips for beach pebbles. We could have summery fruit cups and sparkling juice with miniature paper beach umbrellas. And there'll be a hotdog octopus for everyone."

"It all sounds perfect!" cried Coral.

"And very delicious too," added Nicks.

"Well, I'd better get started then." There

wasn't very much time left, but of course nobody knew this better than Coral's mum. She left right away and was already busy with an imaginary shopping list before her feet had even hit the beach sand. But there was no time for jubilant squealing from the girls. Ruby arrived, breathless with happiness.

"Jake is coming to the party!" she announced. "He really loves the Toys for Africa idea. But I also had to promise to never be involved in trying to set him up again." Now was the perfect moment for jubilant squealing. Well, not quite.

Still, Jake was coming and that was the main thing. And with Jake confirmed for the party, Coral suddenly knew exactly what to do. With Nicks's approval (of course), they would keep Jake a secret from Charlie. They wouldn't tell Jake about Charlie either. They would casually introduce the pair and then stand back and leave them to it. Two was company. Four was officially a crowd.

love is in the air

Summertime in Sunday Harbour was packed full of beautiful sunny days, but the day of the party dawned more glorious than any other. The sky was the clearest blue and seemed to arc around them like a brilliant blue dome. And the air was just right: fresh and warm with a light cool breeze. The sea seemed to be on top form too. The water was clear and calm with small waves curling around the edges.

Even the beach sand seemed softer and smoother than ever before. It really was the most perfect day for a party.

Coral's mum had borrowed trestle tables from the lifeguard's station and dressed each one in a beachy tablecloth. There was a cloth covered in colourful ice-cream cones; another one had different sea creatures like starfish, seahorses and crabs printed across it; and the third one was blue decorated with orange, red and yellow fish in different shapes and sizes. She'd laid the food and drinks out carefully and hired shady umbrellas from Mervin's hut on the beach to keep everything fresh and cool.

Coral Hut looked especially beautiful too. It had been dusted and cleaned till it sparkled. Jake's driftwood wind chimes dangled gracefully and played soft tinkly tunes for everyone to enjoy. And Ruby's garland strings of shells hung everywhere and glittered like small jewels in the pale gold light.

Their guests arrived on time and everyone left their toys for Africa in the large cardboard donation box. Friends found each other and made chit-chat with their bare toes buried in the sand and a drink or snack in their hands. Others wandered inside Coral Hut and cooed over the pretty prints, comfy cushions and dazzling whitewashed walls. And off to the right a group of Sunday Harbour locals played a game of beach football. Or they thought about it, anyway. They had some trouble deciding who would be in which team.

Coral stood behind the trestle table with the ice-cream cones cloth and helped serve drinks to everyone. Her mum poured the juice into cups and Coral added the finishing touches to each one: two cubes of ice and one pop-up paper party umbrella. Romeo hovered close by; the snack tables were just a tail wag away. But he looked torn – food to his right and a football to the left. He stared from one to the other. A hotdog octopus could drop from the tables at any moment, or the game of football might start up.

Nicks stood with Ruby on the deck of Coral Hut and spotted Charlie first. She waved their neighbour over, and noticed that for all of Birdie's enthusiasm and efforts, Charlie was still dressed in long shorts with big old boy pockets and a Star Wars T-shirt. But instead of her usual lace-up boots she was barefoot. And she'd painted her toenails a very pretty shade of pearly pink. So Birdie's moaning and groaning had had some effect on her. Nicks smiled. She was excited and looking forward to Jake's arrival, although of course she didn't tell Charlie that.

It was Coral who spied Jake first. He was carrying a fluffy grey stuffed koala and looked uncomfortable, although whether this was because he was attached to a fluffy toy or because he was worried by what they might do to him this time she couldn't be sure. He gazed around and swung the koala awkwardly. He looked eager to get rid of it. He was searching desperately for the donation box – in the wrong place. But of course only Coral knew this, except she was very busy serving drinks.

Finally he wandered over to the food tables, where he stood for a while and considered the driftwood pretzels thoughtfully. He chose a seashell-shaped chocolate instead and gulped it down. A girl Coral recognised from the lifeguards' station strolled up to the tables. She was tall with long sun-streaked hair that looked really soft and shiny and well brushed. She wore a pretty pink sundress with a matching bag and carried a doll with a dummy under her arm (although she looked less uncomfortable about clutching her toy for Africa than Jake did). She leaned over and helped herself to a marshmallow fish. That was when she clearly noticed the koala bear in Jake's grip. She laughed out loud and said something to Jake while she patted the top of her doll's head. Jake laughed too and shrugged in the direction of his koala bear. Of course Coral couldn't hear what they were saying, but she could tell that feeling silly about carrying toys had become a talking point.

The girl smiled at Jake once more and twirled her hair with her fingers. Her head was now tilted at a slight angle and her right foot had tucked itself behind the left one while she twisted at the hips ever so slightly. Coral had watched enough romantic comedies (one of her favourites was called *Blind Date*) to recognise that this was standard flirty behaviour. But would Jake notice? He suddenly laughed out loud at something the girl with the twirly fingers had said. And he kept on smiling.

Coral's shoulders slumped. This was not how they'd planned it. She considered her next move: should she step in and usher Jake on his way to Charlie and encourage the flirty girl in the other direction? She thought about it for a moment. But if she'd learned one thing, it was that love had a mind of its own – you couldn't control it completely. So, biting down hard on her bottom lip and with her fists clenched so tight they turned bright white, she stayed put. But she did continue to stare at the pair for a little while longer. If she couldn't separate them physically, she would try and separate them with the power of her thoughts.

Jake, shouldn't you be looking for your little sister...?

And flirty girl, your friends will be wondering where you are...

The voice in her head was deep and rather spooky, but neither Jake nor his new friend seemed to hear it.

the course of true love

Two things happened next. First Coral's mum appeared behind the food tables and, with her arms outstretched, offered to deposit the fluffy grey koala bear and the doll with the dummy in the donation box. And just a bit further along – a little closer to the shoreline – two beach football teams slowly started to take shape.

Jake turned to the horizon and noticed the

two groups of football players. Next to sailing, chasing a ball was his favourite thing to do at the beach. He smiled apologetically and waved goodbye to the flirty girl and walked in the direction of the game. The team that seemed to be mostly made up of boys quickly swallowed him up into their fold. They'd seen Jake around before; he was a good, strong player. The other team, which consisted mostly of girls and a few disgruntled-looking boys, scowled and wagged their fingers crossly in the air. They were short of a few players!

Coral saw the moment and seized it. She abandoned the ice cubes and paper umbrellas and scooted over to where Nicks, Charlie and Ruby stood looking out over the deck of Coral Hut.

"Come on girls – how about a game of beach football?" She jiggled her eyebrows knowingly. Charlie had no idea why, but Nicks immediately recognised the look. Her best friend had a plan. And of course it was a fairly obvious one. Jake was tall; he stood out among the rest of the beach football players.

"No thanks, we're just fine," she hissed with a frown. Sporty dates had not worked out for them in the past.

"It'll be great fun – come on," Coral sang brightly.

"It'll get weird," replied Nicks through clenched teeth, although her mouth was still smiling (this was a party, after all). Charlie and Ruby looked confused. They had no idea what was going on, but something was definitely going on.

"No, it won't get weird." Coral smiled.

"Oh, yes, it will." Nicks smiled.

"We need a few more players," broadcast one of the girls playing football to the party crowd. "Do we have any volunteers?" The sprinkling of boys in her team gazed out hopefully at the male party guests.

"Yoo hoo – you've got four more players

over here!" hollered Coral with her hand in the air like this was geography class and she knew the answer.

Nicks scowled. Ruby whooped excitedly and scrambled down the beach hut steps. And Charlie bit her top lip.

"Come on, you lot!" shouted Coral with a laugh as she kicked up sand and skipped over to her brand-new beach football team, which now consisted of a lot of girls and some miserable-looking boys.

Ruby was there in a moment, the other two girls followed reluctantly. A referee was appointed, the whistle blew and the ball was thrown into the middle of the beach football pitch which was marked by lines of evenly spaced flip-flops, trainers, sandals and some pumps. There was even a pair of black flippers.

The mostly-boys' team got control of the ball quickly and zigzagged it in the direction of the mostly-girls' team's goalposts, which consisted of two long sticks sticking out of the sand. They were skilful and nimble; they were definitely regular beach football players. Many of the girls weren't quite as skilled, but they were energetic and determined. Instead of fancy footwork they took careful aim and kicked hard. They protected their goal lines with human chains and created a good defence by waving their hands about wildly and hooting loudly to distract their opponents.

Charlie spent the first few minutes watching and learning the game, and then slowly her frown transformed into a grin. Beach football was not very different from the army. You had two sides. And you had to attack and defend. Even if she didn't have any football skills, she clearly now understood how the game worked.

"Come on, team!" she called out with all the enthusiasm she could muster. "We need more defenders up the left field. And stay behind the ball." She'd worked that out for herself too.

But it was too little, too late. The other team suddenly slammed the ball between the two sticks in the sand and screamed, 'GOAL!' They ran around in circles with their shirts pulled over the heads and hugged each other like this was the World Cup.

But it was only one goal and the other team was now more determined than ever. Charlie rallied the troops with stern words of encouragement and a few barked orders regarding attacking and defensive positions. The Captain watched proudly from the deck of Headquarters.

Jake was next to get hold of the ball. He was quick. And he knew how to move it along, tapping it left, then right, left and right. He glanced up every so often. His eyes were focused on the two sticks in the sand. This was not lost on Charlie; she saw what he was planning. She started running. She crouched lower, using her arms to build up her speed. Her leg muscles pushed against the deep, soft beach sand and her shoulders moved her arms like pistons, driving her forward. She was about to close in on the boy who had the ball (that was really all she knew about him).

All she could think about was her tackle. She threw her body sideways and brought both feet forward at once. They were aimed directly at the ball and her timing was perfect (for a tackle, anyway). It wasn't quite so perfect for Jake. He saw her coming, but he was moving just as fast. He couldn't have stopped even if he'd wanted to. His feet got tangled up in the tackle, but his body kept flying forward and he landed on top of the girl with a loud 'OOMPH!' sound.

For a moment the heap that was made up of Jake on top of Charlie remained silent and unmoving. And then slowly Jake stirred. He curled his back and brought a hand to his lip, which was already bruised and swollen. And then he realised that there was a person trapped beneath him. Quickly he rolled to one side and plopped on to the sand with his hand still pressed to his mouth.

Charlie groaned and sat upright, rubbing the lump on her head that had collided with Jake's jaws.

"Are you all right?" he gurgled through thick lips.

Charlie nodded in a painful sort of way. She would live. And besides, it really was her fault. "Sorry about that," she finally managed. She'd got carried away, but it had sort of happened without her planning it. Succeeding was simply the army way. She inspected the tall boy with big blue eyes and colour co-ordinated lip. It looked like he would live too.

Jake inspected the girl with long dark hair that had been tied in a ponytail but was now half up, half hanging around her pretty oval face. She was trying to appear polite, but her chin was still pushed forward and determined. She was already looking around for the football.

He grinned; he couldn't help it. He wasn't used to lively girls like this one.

Charlie thought he was making fun of her and scowled. *Typical boy – thinking she was nothing more than a silly girl!*

This turned Jake's smile into a short, sharp laugh. This girl really was something else.

"Are you laughing at me?" Charlie demanded to know.

This made Jake laugh even harder, which only made his lip hurt even more. He touched it tenderly and wiped at the tears spurting from his eyes.

Charlie squinted at him suspiciously. And then she started to laugh too. He had a bruised, swollen lip and she had an egg growing on her head – *what a sight they must have made!*

And then suddenly they were surrounded

194

by their team-mates and other people from the party. Coral's mum wanted to know if they were all right. Ruby cuddled up to Jake protectively. Then the Captain arrived with a small torch, which he shone in both their eyes. He seemed unconcerned and pleased with what he saw there.

While all this went on Jake and Charlie simply stared at one other and smiled. Coral left them to it for a few moments. She resisted for as long as she could. But then she couldn't help herself.

"Charlie, this is Jake," she announced. "And Jake, this is Charlie." She smiled at them both in a satisfied sort of way. So fate had stepped in at the last moment and taken over, but the original plan had been hers. She was pleased. Gently she tucked a business card into each of their hands.

A concerned-looking Ruby was now stroking Jake's head. Charlie glanced from the little girl to Jake and back again. She didn't say anything at first; she was putting all the pieces together in her head. And then her eyes lit up.

"Are you the Jake who made the driftwood wind chimes?" she asked.

Jake glanced up at the dangling shells swaying and tinkling in the sea breeze and grinned. And then he grimaced. He'd forgotten about his lip. He nodded instead.

"They're so beautiful!" Charlie sighed.

Jake shrugged bashfully.

"No, really," she gushed, "I could never make anything like that."

"You probably could if I showed you how."

Charlie paused for a nervous gulp. "You would?"

He shrugged again. "Sure."

"How about I get you an icepack for your lip first?" Army life had taught her how to handle most emergency situations.

Jake nodded and smiled. Only he didn't seem to mind how much it hurt this time.

They both stood up on wobbly legs and zigzagged their way over to the bucket of ice behind the trestle table still covered in the cloth of colourful ice-cream cones. Coral's business cards lay abandoned on the sand, quite forgotten. Nicks leaned down and picked one up. Her eyebrows rose higher with every word she read.

CORAL OF CORAL HUT
THE CUPID COMPANY
MANAGING DIRECTOR AND EXECUTIVE
PRESIDENT IN CHARGE OF OPERATIONS
ALL FOR LOVE AND LOVE FOR ALL

It was the busiest business card in the history of business cards. She returned them to her crazy friend and shook her head.

"Executive President in Charge of Operations?" she repeated, and squished her face up like it was moon speak and made absolutely no sense to her.

"You can be an executive president in charge of operations too if you like," replied Coral with an unconcerned bounce of her shoulders.

"I'm not even sure I know what it means," said Nicks.

"Well, then you shouldn't let it bother you one bit."

"I still don't know why we need fancy titles."

Coral rolled her eyes at this. She'd already explained about McDonalds and Nike once before. She was about to go through it again when Ruby grabbed her hand and started pulling. She was pulling Nicks along in the same way.

"Come on, you two!" The smaller girl chuckled. "This is a party – remember?"

all for love and love for all

The partygoers stayed on until the early evening. And only then did they begin to leave the beach in small lively groups. The day's warm sunshine and excitement had flushed everyone's cheeks bright pink. Their eyes were sparkly but hanging at half-mast – they were all tired, but very happy. The party had been a success. Strangers had made friends, friends had shared in the fun, and everyone felt carefree and summery – Coral and Nicks especially.

They lolled on their deckchairs and watched the sun begin its slow, steady slide down the sky. Coral's mum was talking with Birdie on the deck next door. Actually, she wasn't talking as much as listening. Birdie was still deliriously thrilled about the fact that Charlie seemed to be paying attention to a boy. She twittered away to Coral's mum, glancing down every so often at the girl and boy sitting on the blanket on the beach just a short distance in front of the huts. Jake had Ruby's bag of shells and a roll of fishing gut and was patiently showing Charlie how to thread the shells on to strings. The driftwood part would come later; the creative process could not be rushed.

Neither Coral nor Nicks spoke for a while. They were both just enjoying the afterglow of a very triumphant day. Not only had it been the best day ever, but they'd finally racked up a score for the Cupid Company. And it felt good.

Romeo had enjoyed the day too. He'd also found love. Hotdog octopuses were now his absolute favourite treat in the entire world. They were even better with a blob of barbecue sauce, if he could get it (which was a lot easier when Coral's mum wasn't around). But with the food eaten and the leftovers packed away there was nothing left for him to do but nap, and that's exactly what he did on the top step of Coral Hut's deck.

"You know, I think we learned one very important lesson today," Coral finally spoke.

"And what's that?" Nicks kept her eyes closed and her head pressed against the back of her deckchair.

"That love has a mind of its own; you really can't force it to do anything."

This thing called love and Coral really had quite a lot in common then. Nicks smiled but kept her thoughts to herself. Her eyes were still shut as she listened to the rush of the waves on the beach sand.

But Coral had never been one for resting her eyes. She was still feeling lively; the memory of their brilliant day kept her buzzing with energy. Coral Hut had been the best thing that had ever happened to them. They now had their own special little place in the world. They'd met some nice new people too. She glanced over at Charlie and Jake and her mum chatting to Birdie on the deck of Headquarters. They were a small, rather chummy community.

She turned and squinted at the glossy red hut – their neighbour on the other side of Coral Hut. They'd been so busy she'd never really given it much thought until that moment: but they still hadn't met this neighbour. They hadn't even seen this neighbour! And yet summer was already well on its way. The glossy red hut's doors looked like they were locked up tight, and its shutters remained closed and latched. She gave a small shrug; there was still plenty of summertime left to meet everyone. This made her smile. She loved the long warm days spent at the beach. There was always so much to see and do.

Now that the beach was emptying, juniors from the lifeguards' station had arrived carrying yellow plastic kayaks between them. Some carried oars too and they were all padded out with luminous lifejackets. Coral watched them wading out into knee-deep water and giggled quietly as they tried to climb into the plastic kayaks without tipping.

One boy managed to remain upright for a few seconds. He floated for a short while and then tipped sideways and reappeared on the other side of the kayak. He bobbed to the surface with his hair plastered to his head, spewing a fountain of salt water from his mouth. The other junior lifeguards laughed so hard they also tipped sideways into the water. There really was a lot of foam and splashing about, but very little of this was created by the oars dipping into the ocean. The two senior lifeguards in charge did not look impressed, and blew fiercely into their whistles. But the girls never actually heard the shrill shriek of the whistles.

"Nicks! Coral!" was all they heard. Somebody was calling out their names very loudly.

They both sat upright with their spines stretched straight, turning their heads left then right like two nosy ferrets. Nicks's mum was charging up the beach and waving a bit of paper in the air. Her eyes were big and shiny and her cheeks were red with the effort of dashing at top speed.

"Look what I have here!" she shouted, and waved the bit of paper so briskly it looked like it was caught in a sea squall. She really was very excited about something. Even Romeo sat up and pricked his ears forward. He sniffed the air to check if the excitement had anything to do with food. Doggy instinct told him it did not, so he went back to sleep again.

Nicks waved to her mum from the deck.

Coral jumped up and hopped about. "What is it?" she hollered back through cupped hands.

But Nicks's mum was too tired to call out any more. She arrived panting, and took a few moments to slow her breathing. "This," she finally spoke, "is from the Royal Navy. It's a reply to the letter you sent asking about Third Officer Perry Philips."

The girls suddenly turned to each other and stared with big egg eyes. They were unexpectedly nervous about opening the letter. They shared another brief, silent best-friend conversation:

Finally, a reply!

But what if they have no record of Third Officer Perry Philips?

Exactly – what do we do then?

We owe it to Great-Aunt Coral to pass the letters on.

We have to try our best!

We'll travel to the ends of the earth if we have to and spend our lifetimes dedicated to this mission of love. Because romance rules!

Of course this last bit was from Coral. It was just like her to get carried away with the moment. Nicks sighed and turned to face her mum.

"You open the letter," she pleaded.

Nicks's mum nodded and composed her face so that she looked calm and collected. She knew all about Great-Aunt Coral and Third Officer Perry Philips. She realised that this was a big moment for the girls. She'd also known Great-Aunt Coral, and returning the old love letters to their rightful owner also meant something to her. She coughed to clear her voice and began reading.

"*Dear Madams, thank you for your recent enquiry regarding one of our esteemed Royal*

Navy men, Third Officer Perry Philips."

Hearing his name spoken out loud was something (it may have been Nicks's mum's voice but in their hearts and heads the words echoed all the way from Royal Navy headquarters). For a moment both girls imagined deep-sea submarines and giant metal ships filled with Royal Navy men and women looking brave and neat dressed in their blue and white uniforms with sharp hats and shiny badges and dripping medals. They imagined the men and women saluting and marching and winning battles in the name of their country. They sighed (Coral a little more loudly).

Nicks's mum had also been enjoying an imagination moment and she paused a few moments before continuing.

"Having consulted our records we can confirm that Third Officer Philips was drafted aboard the HMS Bulwark during the Cold War. He was listed as a member of the vessel's

crew when it was officially reported missing in the northern Atlantic Ocean on 17th June 1949. The ship remained missing at sea until it was discovered sunk off the coast of Greenland in 1951. There were no survivors of this tragedy, although bodies of some of the Royal Navy seamen were recovered. Third Officer Philips was amongst these. Following the wishes of his family he was laid to rest at Cabot's Cove Cemetery. Third Officer Philips gave his life for his country and will always be remembered and honoured as a hero."

Nicks's mum stopped reading and glanced up from the letter. For a few moments none of them spoke. They used the time to absorb the letter's words and meaning instead. And very soon each one had shiny, wet eyes.

Nicks was the first to speak. "Great-Aunt Coral's letters are all dated between 1949 and 1951…" she considered thoughtfully.

Coral finished the sentence for her. "… this was when Perry Philips and the *HMS Bulwark* were officially missing at sea."

"She had no idea where to find him," choked Coral.

"That's why she couldn't send her letters to him."

"But she loved him so much she kept on writing."

"It was all she had…"

"Do you think that's why she came to Coral Hut," wondered Coral, "to watch the sea and wait for him?"

Nicks's mum reached out and rubbed the girls' arms gently. They finally had their answer, but it didn't leave them quite as happy as they'd thought it would. Great-Aunt Coral had hoped to spend the rest of her life with Perry Philips. But he'd never made it back to her alive. And still she'd waited, never marrying someone else or daring to leave the one place she knew he might find her.

"Maybe they're finally together now," said Coral with a small sob.

Nicks's mum folded the letter and returned it to its envelope printed with the Royal Navy seal. "We can still take her letters to him," she said.

The girls looked up sadly.

"I know where to find Cabot's Cove Cemetery. It's not too far from Sunday Harbour. But first we'll need one strong waterproof, weatherproof container for the letters."

The girls thought about this for a moment. And then their dull, droopy eyes grew wider and brighter. They understood exactly what they needed to do.

"We have the perfect thing," announced Coral before disappearing inside the beach hut. Nicks followed her and very soon both girls returned to Nicks's mum on the deck – Coral carrying her great-aunt's empty cake tin covered in cherry blossoms and Nicks clutching the pile of love letters to Perry Philips.

They smiled at each other. They were a team. Coral popped open the cake tin and Nicks laid the letters carefully inside. Coral placed the lid back on the cake tin and they both tapped it three times for luck.

Nicks's mum sighed brightly. "That's set then. We could leave for Cabot's Cove first thing tomorrow morning. Coral, you'll have to check with your mum first, of course."

Coral glanced over at her mum, who was now slumped in a chair on the deck of Headquarters. She was still listening to Birdie, who still seemed to be chattering away and making grand hand and arm gestures. It looked like she was demonstrating 'big old boy pockets'.

Coral's mum caught Coral's eye and sent her a secret wink and a smile. She didn't mind getting caught up in Birdie's nattering. She then noticed Nicks's mum standing with the girls and called out and waved her over.

A strong wind had come up and it tossed

her words about, making them very difficult to catch. Nicks's mum turned her head so that her right ear was an inch or two closer but it was no good – it still sounded like Coral's mum wanted to introduce her to a bird.

"Hold on, I'll come over," she called out to Coral's mum before turning back to Coral. "I'll mention our trip to Cabot's Cove, shall I?" Coral nodded her thanks. "Great, it'll be an adventure. And well done, girls – for the love letters and for a fabulous day." And then she was gone, heading for Headquarters.

Suddenly there was a loud thud. The girls spun in the direction of the noise. It seemed to have come from the glossy red hut next door, which still appeared to be locked up tight. Was there somebody inside? But they hadn't seen anyone go in. All of a sudden there was another noise. This time it sounded like a chair scraping. The girls turned to each other. Coral jiggled her eyebrows.

"Could that be our next Cupid Company victim then?"

Nicks smiled. "I'm ready when you are!"

Coral turned back to the red hut and considered their next candidate. They'd already helped one neighbour find love and happiness. And of course they were ready to help anybody else who might be lonely and loveless in Sunday Harbour. As Managing Directors (plus one Executive President in Charge of Operations) of the Cupid Company, by the time they were done, it really would be *all for love and love for all*!

More cute and crazy fun as The Cupid Company faces its biggest challenge yet!

A group of glamorous, snobby teenagers has moved in to the beach hut next door. The girls think that no guys are good enough for them – but Coral and Nicks have other ideas!

Turn over for a sneak preview…

The sky above the girl curved like the inside of a giant beach ball. It then dipped and faded to blue before gently dissolving into the ocean's horizon. She squinted at the edge of the world, her red-brown hair, curled like a head of bedsprings, bobbed around her. The horizon definitely looked like the edge of the world. It was the edge of her world anyway – a long way off.

She scanned the enormous sandpit before her. The beach was full of children with their buckets and spades, making shapes out of the soft, warm sand. A boy dripping wet from head to toe raced out of the sea before flopping, belly-first, onto a patch of dry sand. He then rolled left and right until every inch of him was bitty and yellow before tiptoeing up to where a woman stood waiting to catch a Frisbee. Before she could do anything to stop him he had given her a full-body hug. She yelped. He laughed gleefully.

The sky above was suddenly filled with a whirring sound and an airplane flew across the sky with a long canvas tail that seemed to flick and ripple in the wind. The girl stared with a wrinkled nose until the airplane was almost overhead. The canvas tail had a message: BEST OF LUCK SARA AND JEFF... LOTS OF LOVE.

The airplane continued on its way, as if to the sun, pulling the flying message across the sky. The girl shook her head. She was suddenly annoyed. Just *who* had wished Sara and Jeff the best of luck? Would Sara and Jeff know?

"Coral? Coral, can you hear me?"

The girl turned toward her best friend. "Mmm?"

"You actually have to move the broom to make a difference."

Coral stared at the broom she held like a dance partner in her arms. There was a dent in her forehead from where she'd been resting her head against it. Her friend was right; she hadn't done much sweeping. The thing was – she hated sweeping the beach hut. Unfortunately her friend, Nicks, hated sweeping too. So every week they were taking it in turns. It just always felt like it was her turn.

"What's the hurry, Nicks?" Coral grumbled.

Suddenly, and without warning, there was a loud thump-whack sound coming from the glossy red beach hut next door.

Both girls' heads spun in the direction of

the hut. They stared, silent and blinking.

"Did you hear that?" whispered Coral.

"Oh yes." Nicks's reply sounded like a hiss.

"We didn't imagine it then?"

Nicks shook her head slowly. This wasn't the first time they'd heard strange noises coming from the neighbouring glossy red beach hut either. And yet they had never ever (ever) seen a single soul enter or leave the place. It was always locked up tight with its shutters closed like two sleeping eyes.

Just then a shadow flitted across the window, and then it was gone.

"Did you see that?" gasped Coral, although her lips hardly moved at all. She felt like she was being watched, but she didn't want the watcher to know this.

Nicks nodded and gulped. She had definitely seen that.

They both stood still and silent, staring – almost wishing for another sight or sound because that could possibly offer some perfectly obvious explanation as to what they'd just seen and heard.

They stood for a while longer when all of a sudden a dog started yapping. Both girls jumped like they'd been electrocuted. It was Romeo, Coral's Jack Russell pup.

"Romeo!" they both groaned aloud. Romeo took his guard dog duties very seriously.

"We're probably just being silly," said Nicks. "I'm sure the noises aren't anything." Nicks had always being a sensible sort of girl. She'd never been the type to get tangled up in an overactive imagination and she didn't want to start now.

"But I definitely heard and saw something," insisted Coral.

Nicks shrugged.

"It's not the first time we've heard strange noises coming from the red hut either."

"It's the first time we've *seen* anything strange though," replied Nicks reasonably.

"So what should we do about it? Who should we tell?" said Coral.

"Tell about what?" sighed Nicks. "We've no proof that there's anything strange going on. OK, we've heard a few noises... So what?"

That was true. Coral thought a bit more about this. She really wasn't the type to let a dramatic moment pass by unnoticed, but Nicks had a point: apart from a thump-whack and a vague shadow, what else did they really have?

"So what should we do?" she asked instead.

"We should finish cleaning the beach hut and then concentrate on Cupid Company business," replied Nicks sensibly.

Coral nodded. Of course Nicks was right. Cupid Company business should always come first. After all, it was what the hut was all about now.

Coral had inherited the hut from her Great Aunt Coral, but it wasn't long before it had become more than just a beach hut and had become home to the little business that they had set up – the business of love and matchmaking. And so far, they'd had two success strikes – Cousin Archie and Gwyn, and Charlie (daughter of the next-door beach hut owners) and Jake.

Coral sighed dreamily. The true path of love could be a lot of fun. Still, for now, she'd better get on with sweeping up. It was her mum who had issued strict instructions to keep the hut clean and tidy at all times. Maturity and responsibility – that's what it took to keep the hut, she had said. And her mum usually meant what she said too.

Coral reached for her dancing partner, the broom, and sighed. Acting cool, calm and collected did not come naturally to her. Still, she would try her best to concentrate on Cupid Company business while she was sweeping the sand from the deck of Coral Hut, which was how she came to realise that *there* was *no Cupid Company business!* Quickly she pointed this out to Nicks.

"*No business* is the Cupid Company business we need to concentrate on," came Nicks's reply.

"Of course it is," mumbled Coral while she kept one eye trained on the sandiest corner of the deck. She would keep her promise to her mum, but she wouldn't take her other eye off the glossy red beach hut either. Something exciting could happen and she wasn't going to miss it!